Samuel French Acting Edition

Murder For Two

by Joe Kinosian
and Kellen Blair

SAMUELFRENCH.COM   SAMUELFRENCH.CO.UK

FOR PRODUCTION ENQUIRIES

UNITED STATES AND CANADA
Info@SamuelFrench.com
1-866-598-8449

UNITED KINGDOM AND EUROPE
Plays@SamuelFrench.co.uk
020-7255-4302

Each title is subject to availability from Samuel French, depending upon country of performance. Please be aware that *MURDER FOR TWO* may not be licensed by Samuel French in your territory. Professional and amateur producers should contact the nearest Samuel French office or licensing partner to verify availability.

MUSIC USE NOTE

Licensees are solely responsible for obtaining formal written permission from copyright owners to use copyrighted music in the performance of this play and are strongly cautioned to do so. If no such permission is obtained by the licensee, then the licensee must use only original music that the licensee owns and controls. Licensees are solely responsible and liable for all music clearances and shall indemnify the copyright owners of the play(s) and their licensing agent, Samuel French, against any costs, expenses, losses and liabilities arising from the use of music by licensees. Please contact the appropriate music licensing authority in your territory for the rights to any incidental music.

IMPORTANT BILLING AND CREDIT REQUIREMENTS

If you have obtained performance rights to this title, please refer to your licensing agreement for important billing and credit requirements.

MURDER FOR TWO received its world premiere production on May 17, 2011 at Chicago Shakespeare Theater, Chicago, Illinois (Barbara Gaines, Artistic Director, Criss Henderson, Executive Director). *MURDER FOR TWO* was developed for Chicago Shakespeare Theater by Rick Boynton, Creative Producer. It was directed by David H. Bell; the set design was by Scott Davis; the costume design was by Jeremy W. Floyd; the lighting design was by Jesse Klug; the sound design was by James Savage; the music direction was by Roberta Duchak; and the production stage manager was Claire E. Zawa. The cast was as follows:

MARCUS MOSCOWICZ . . . . Alan Schmuckler
THE SUSPECTS . . . . Joe Kinosian

MURDER FOR TWO received its New York premiere production on July 25, 2013 at Second Stage Theatre Uptown (Carole Rothman, Artistic Director, Casey Reitz, Executive Director, Christopher Burney, Curator and Associate Artistic Director) and was subsequently transferred to New World Stages with an official opening on November 6, 2013, produced by Jayson Raitt, Barbara Whitman, Steven Chaikelson, and Second Stage Theatre. It was directed by Scott Schwartz; the set design was by Beowulf Boritt; the costume design was by Andrea Lauer; the lighting design was by Jason Lyons; the sound design was by Jill BC Du Boff; the music direction was by David Caldwell; the choreography was by Wendy Seyb; and the production stage managers were Lori Ann Zepp (Second Stage) and Amber White (New World Stages). The cast was as follows:

MARCUS MOSCOWICZ . . . . Brett Ryback
THE SUSPECTS . . . . Jeff Blumenkrantz

MURDER FOR TWO was developed at the Adirondack Theatre Festival, during the 2010 Season.

CHARACTERS

One actor portrays:

MARCUS MOSCOWICZ – an ambitious young officer,
and provides voices for two characters in flashback:

THE CHIEF – Marcus's grizzled boss, and

VANESSA – Marcus's former partner.

The other actor portrays:

THE SUSPECTS

DAHLIA WHITNEY – the victim's loopy widow,

MURRAY & **BARB FLANDON** – the Whitneys' bickering neighbors,

STEPH WHITNEY – an overeager grad student,

BARRETTE LEWIS – a self-incriminating ballerina,

DR. GRIFF – a friendly local psychiatrist,

TIMMY, YONKERS & **SKID** – members of an antiquated boys' choir, and

HENRY VIVALDI – a late arrival.

The final character is **OFFICER LOU**, who isn't played by an actor.
Marcus and The Suspects address him as needed.

SETTING

An isolated mansion in rural New England

TIME

Present day

AUTHOR'S NOTE

MURDER FOR TWO is performed by two piano-playing actors, and is intended to be performed with minimal, if any, production elements. The only necessary set piece is a piano in the middle of the room on which the actors accompany themselves and one another.

ON AD LIBBING

The play should have the feel of being improvised on the spot without any actual ad libbing taking place. Two notable exceptions: if at any time during a performance an audience member's cell phone rings or a person is caught texting / e-mailing, don't let it pass by unnoticed. By all means have the characters of Marcus and (especially) Dahlia insult / embarrass them ad lib, as in Dahlia's speech on p. 55. The other ad libbing exception is in the Henry Vivaldi section; it's permissible for The Suspects to try and throw Marcus for a loop by using different accents and physicalizations without altering the lines themselves.

SONG LIST

"Prelude / Waiting in the Dark"
"Protocol Says"
"Protocol Says (Reprise)"
"A Perfectly Lovely Surprise"
"So..."
"It Was Her"
"A Lot Woise"
"He Needs a Partner"
"So What if I Did?"
"A Friend Like You"
"A Friend Like You (Reprise)"
"Henry Vivaldi"
"Process of Elimination"
"Steppin' Out of the Shadows"
"Finale (I Need a Partner / Protocol Says)"
"Finale Ultimo (A Friend Like You)"

[MUSIC NO. 01 "PRELUDE / WAITING IN THE DARK"]

(**MARCUS** *and* **THE SUSPECTS** *enter and silently prep the stage. In previous versions, this included the introduction of a small, spooky-looking mansion [it could be a dollhouse / model, a shadow, or whatever works best in the space].)*

(**MARCUS** *then begins to play the prelude.* **THE SUSPECTS** *joins him and start goofing off on the piano, much to* **MARCUS***'s chagrin.)*

(**MARCUS** *bumps* **THE SUSPECTS** *out of the way to play lower.)*

(Sound effect: Ravens.)

(At the end, **THE SUSPECTS** *leaps off the piano bench to become* **DAHLIA WHITNEY***.)*

DAHLIA. Okay everybody, the birthday boy'll be here any minute and we can't let him know we're here. So would somebody kill the lights?

(Lights out with a crash of thunder.)

Thanks.

WE'RE WAITING IN THE DARK FOR ARTHUR WHITNEY
EV'RYBODY'S FAV'RITE LOCAL PATRIARCH
EXPECTING HIS APPEARANCE, WE'RE ALL HERE INSIDE
A SPOOKY MANSION WHERE WE'RE WAITING IN THE
    DARK

(We hear the sound of a car.)

Shh! He's here!

(**THE SUSPECTS** *circles in through the door as* **MURRAY** *and* **BARB***.)*

MURRAY. No, it's just us.

BARB. Sorry we're late.

DAHLIA. Quiet, you two. Hurry up and hide!

WE MUSTN'T MAKE A PEEP OR EVEN COUGH NOW;
MURRAY.

WOULDN'T WANNA RUIN THE SURPRISE IN STORE*
BARB.

SO TAKE OUT ALL YOUR PHONES AND TURN THEM OFF
NOW

DAHLIA.

IF YOU HAVE A PAGER, THERE'S A GARBAGE BY THE
DOOR**

(*The sound of another car.*)

Shh! This is definitely him!

STEPH. No, it's just the rest of us. We carpooled. Come on
in you guys.

(**THE SUSPECTS** *circles through the door as*
BARRETTE *and* **DR. GRIFF,** *and then back in as*
DAHLIA.)

DAHLIA. So wait a second: who was hiding in the dark when
this song started? Was it just me? Well that's stupid.

DR. GRIFF.

HE REALLY SHOULD BE HERE BY NOW, OR NEARBY
STEPH.

WOW, THIS ENDLESS WAITING REALLY LEAVES ITS MARK
BARRETTE.

IT ISN'T WHAT WE PLANNED, STILL, WE'LL STILL STAND
STILL

MURRAY.

TILL WE HEAR HIM COMING FROM HIS DAY OF DAILY
LABORS

---

* Alternate lyric: **Murray.** Good old Arthur Whitney's never late, we
know.
** Alternate lyric: **Dahlia.** Basic'ly just act like you're about to see a show.

BARB.

IN OUR QUAINT AND COZY TOWN WHERE EV'RY PERSON
KNOWS THEIR NEIGHBORS

DR. GRIFF.

TO THIS ISOLATED MANSION, QUITE THE GLOOMIEST OF
PLACES

STEPH.

WHERE THE HOUSE IS FULL OF TENSION

DAHLIA.

NOT TO MENTION WEARY FACES
WHO ARE WAITING IN THE –

(The sound of a third car. **DAHLIA** *gasps
excitedly.)*

MARCUS.

OOH...

BARB.

WAIT, I THINK HE'S COMING

DR. GRIFF.

YEAH, I HEAR HIM COMING

MARCUS.

HMM...

DAHLIA.

SHH! HE'LL HEAR US HUMMING
HE'S COMING

(Door opens.)

ALL. Surpri –!

(A gunshot. Beat.)

STEPH. Um...what was that?

(Lights up.)

DAHLIA. There's been a *murrrderrr*!

**[MUSIC NO. 02 "MARCUS'S ENTRANCE
(UNDERSCORE)"]**

*(***THE SUSPECTS*** *takes over at the piano for*
MARCUS, *who has become* **OFFICER MARCUS**

MOSCOWICZ. *He approaches the door of the mansion, talking on his cell phone.)*

MARCUS. *(Into phone.)* Got it, Chief! I'll keep an eye on the suspects till Detective Grayson gets here. After all, protocol says a watchful eye is – okay, Chief. Over and out.

(He's about to ring the doorbell when something startles him.)

Lou! You startled me. Jeez, sneaking up on an officer at the scene of a crime. You're the wackiest cop in New England.

(Beat.)

The chief? Yeah, he just called. Said Detective Grayson is about an hour away.

(Beat.)

Yes, Lou, it looks like he *did* pick the wrong weekend to travel about an hour away. Of course, how could he have foreseen the murder of Arthur Whitney, great American novelist?

(Beat.)

I don't know, Lou, it's hard to pick a favorite. He wrote so many wonderful books. As far I can remember there was only one that filled me with a burning hatred.

(Beat, laughs.)

But that's a story for another day. I will tell you one thing though, my wacky little friend: it's nice having someone to talk to for a change. Why, if you weren't here, I'd just be thinking these things! Don't get me wrong. I didn't say we were partners. I haven't had a partner since... Vanessa.

(Beat, looks serious, then laughs.)

Aw well. I'm better off alone. A partner was only standing between me and, well...

*(**MARCUS** produces a badge from his pocket.)*

...this! Oh, it's just a little badge I had made to remind me of my lifelong dream. "Detective Marcus." It'll happen, Lou, sooner than you think. I overheard the chief saying he's getting ready to promote one of the newbies. Whichever one of us proves to know the most about crime scene protocol. Oh, you don't think I know the most about protocol?

[MUSIC NO. 03 "PROTOCOL SAYS"]

MARCUS. Fine, I'll give you a demonstration. But first let me accidentally pocket-dial the chief so he can overhear this.

(**MARCUS** *bangs his hand against his pocket.*)

PROTOCOL SAYS
BE STRICT
KEEP YOUR COOL OR YOU'LL BE LICKED
NEVER LOOK WEAK
NEVER LOOK HURT
NEVER LOOK A THING EXCEPT ALERT
PROTOCOL SAYS
BE BOLD
KEEP YOUR SUSPECTS WELL CONTROLLED
WHEN YOU'RE IN A PINCH
NEVER GIVE AN INCH
IT CAN BE A CINCH
IF YOU FOLLOW EACH RULE YOU'RE TOLD

EV'RY PUZZLE PIECE HOLDS A CLUE
WHEN YOU'RE ADDING 'EM UP, JUST DO AS PROTOCOL
    SAYS
THEY'LL FALL IN PLACE
EV'RY FINGERPRINT FITS A HAND
IF YOU'RE WILLING TO UNDERSTAND WHAT PROTOCOL
    SAYS
YOU'LL CRACK THE CASE

(Into phone.) Oh my God, Chief, have you been listening this whole time? How embarrassing.

(Beat.)

What? Oh. Well, is the chief available? Can you put him on? Great, thanks.

> (**MARCUS** *stuffs his phone back into his pocket.*)

PROTOCOL SAYS
BE STERN
MAKE THE CRIME YOUR PRIME CONCERN
NEVER LOOK BACK
NEVER THINK TWICE
NEVER LET A SUSPECT GIVE ADVICE
PROTOCOL SAYS
BE SKILLED
DON'T LET MASS COMMOTION BUILD
WHEN IT'S GETTING TOUGH
AND YOU'VE HAD ENOUGH
IF YOU KNOW YOUR STUFF
YOU CAN MANAGE TO NOT GET KILLED

EV'RY ALIBI MUST BE CRACKED
WHEN YOU'RE TRACKING YOUR MAN, JUST ACT AS
    PROTOCOL SAYS
THEY'LL LAND IN JAIL
EV'RY RIDDLE REQUIRES A KEY
IF YOU WANT IT UNLOCKED, JUST SEE WHAT PROTOCOL
    SAYS
AND YOU'LL PREVAIL

(Into phone.) Oh my God, Chief, have you been listening this whole time? How embarrassing.

> *(Short beat.)*

Well, do you know how long his meeting is supposed to last? Fine, give me his voicemail.

> (**MARCUS** *stuffs his phone back into his pocket.*)

Now, protocol says: know the people you're dealing with. I think if we just peek through this window here...aha!

(While **MARCUS** *looks through the window,* **THE SUSPECTS** *becomes the characters being described.)*

I can see...local psychiatrist, Dr. Griff.

(Beat.)

Feisty old couple fighting over a piece of pie.

(Beat.)

Dead body lying next to – wait a second – a gun in the middle of the room! I found the murder weapon! Man, protocol is awesome! Nothing could throw me –

(Beat.)

Oh my gosh, that's Barrette Lewis, the famous prima ballerina. What's a beautiful, innocent soul like her doing here? That's right, I guess we *will* find out.

(Beat.)

How dare you, Lou. I don't care if she *is* the kind of woman that could really help a guy learn to love again. I think we both know what protocol says about mixing your personal and professional lives. That's right, never. Again.

PROTOCOL SAYS
BE SMART
TRUST YOUR GUT AND NOT YOUR HEART
NEVER LOOK FRAIL
NEVER LOOK FLUSHED
NEVER LET YOUR HEART GET CAUGHT, THEN CRUSHED
PROTOCOL SAYS
SAY NO
IF, BY CHANCE, ROMANCE SHOULD GROW
EVEN WHEN THEY SEEM
LIKE A LIVING DREAM
SILKIER THAN CREAM
WITH A PAIR A' PERFECT EYES THAT GLEAM AND GLOW...
BUT THAT WAS LONG AGO
SO VERY LONG AGO

SIX MONTHS LAST WEEK, TO BE EXACT

AND NOW, LOU, I'M READY
RESOLVED, PREPPED, AND STEADY
MY STEADFAST DEVOTION
WILL EARN THAT PROMOTION
NO THREATS WILL DERAIL ME
FOR RULES NEVER FAIL ME
AND STAUNCH DEDICATION
TO STRICT REGULATION HAS SHOWN

EV'RY PUZZLE PIECE HOLDS A CLUE
WHEN YOU'RE ADDING 'EM UP, JUST DO AS PROTOCOL
    SAYS
YOU'LL SOON SUCCEED

TAKE IT, LOU!

> *(Listens to* **LOU**.*)*

THAT'S RIGHT!

PROTOCOL WORKS
PROTOCOL PAYS
PEOPLE MIGHT LEAVE BUT PROTOCOL STAYS
IT'S THE ONLY PARTNERSHIP I...

Oh my God, Chief, have I been leaving you a voicemail this whole time? How embarrassing. Have a great day!

> *(Winks at* **LOU** *and hangs up.)*

IT'S THE ONLY PARTNERSHIP I NEED!

> *(On the final two chords of the song,* **MARCUS** *rings the doorbell. He waits for a moment, smiling professionally back at* **LOU**, *then rings the doorbell again.* **THE SUSPECTS** *gets up from the piano, becomes* **DAHLIA WHITNEY**, *the victim's loopy, attention-starved widow.* **DAHLIA** *hobbles over to open the door.)*

DAHLIA. Yes?

MARCUS. Evening, ma'am, I'm with the Collarhorn Police Department.

MARCUS.	DAHLIA.
This is Officer Lou. We've been sent to keep an eye on... No, ma'am...well, if you'd listen –	Oh, sure! You must be the detective they sent to solve the murder of m'husband. So glad you could make it! I'm Dahlia Whitney. You know, the victim's wife.

MARCUS. We're so sorry for your loss, but I'm actually –

DAHLIA. Did you know my husband?

MARCUS. Only by reputation.

DAHLIA. Course he's not my husband, anymore...he's God's husband now.

MARCUS.	DAHLIA.
(Uncertain.) Yes.	On account a' being dead.
(Beat.)	

DAHLIA. You wanna come in?

MARCUS. Sure, thank you.

> (**MARCUS** *follows* **DAHLIA** *inside and trips over something unseen.*)

DAHLIA. Watch the body there.

> (**MARCUS** *kneels down to inspect it.*)

MARCUS. Shot in the forehead.

DAHLIA. Mm-hmm.

MARCUS. Hey, what about these books, Mrs. Whitney? There has to be at least twenty of them scattered around the body. Including a first edition of *Scattered Around the Body.* I love this book.

DAHLIA. Isn't that the one where the novelist husband gets shot in the head?

> *(Starts crying.)*

It's amazing how the most random things can remind you of your personal troubles. Poor guy. Didn't even have a chance to finish *All of Them Bananas.*

MARCUS. Excuse me?

DAHLIA. His next book, *All of Them Bananas*. Leave it to Arthur to cash in on the banana craze, Detective.

MARCUS. I'm not the –

DAHLIA. Detective! That's what you are: the detective. And since you're here, Detective, maybe you can figure out who committed the *other* crime.

MARCUS. Other crime?

DAHLIA. Yeah, on top of everything else...someone stole the ice cream!

MARCUS. I see.

DAHLIA. So you're probably gonna need to meet the other guests, right?

MARCUS.	**DAHLIA.**
Yes, good idea, thank you Mrs. Whitney, if you don't mind, Officer Lou and I – yes – okay, thank you!	Sure. Sure. Sure. That makes sense. Good detective! I'll introduce you to all the suspects, I mean guests, I mean suspects!

(**DAHLIA** *turns as if she's about to start walking, then suddenly faces front again.*)

DAHLIA. Ta-da!

MARCUS. What?

DAHLIA. Well, everybody's been sittin' here the whole time, Detective.

MARCUS. Gah!

DAHLIA. Say hello.

MARCUS. Hello folks.

MURRAY. Evening.

BARB. Hi!

DR. GRIFF. Howdy!

STEPH. Hey...

BARRETTE. Hello.

MARCUS.

I'm Marcus Moscowicz with the Collarhorn Police Department, and this is Officer Lou. We're here to keep an eye – no. No.

No, that's not true!

DAHLIA.

This is that detective they sent to find out which one of you killed the birthday boy. So look out, he's the detective! The detective!

DAHLIA. You're gonna love him.

MARCUS. Listen, everybody; Mrs. Whitney is a little confused. I'm not... I'm not the...

MURRAY. Not the what?

[MUSIC NO. 04 "PROTOCOL SAYS (REPRISE)"]

Come now, Detective, hurry up and solve the crime!

MARCUS.

PROTOCOL SAYS...

BARB. Come to think of it, there hasn't been a murder in Collarhorn for years. Be a big deal for whoever solves it.

MARCUS.

BE STRONG

DAHLIA. Talk about something that'll impress the chief. Ya know, if that's like a thing you're worried about.

MARCUS.

DON'T LET PASSION STEER YOU WRONG

BARRETTE. What were you saying, Detective? You're not the...?

MARCUS. Uh, yes... I'm not the detective...

(*Beat.*)

That usually works this district. But since Detective Grayson is out of town...

(**MARCUS** *steps aside.*)

(*Whispering.*) Listen, Lou, just give me until Grayson shows up; that's fifty-two minutes. I know I can solve this; I'm great at this stuff! I started reading *Ten Little Indians* and immediately knew the judge did it.

> *(Beat.)*

Oh, you haven't? The judge did it. Come on, Lou. This is my chance to show the chief I've got what it takes.

> *(Beat, smiles.)*

Thanks.

> *(Beat, to the room.)*

Yes, I'm Detective Marcus. And I'm here to solve the mystery of who killed Arthur Whitney.

DAHLIA. And the other mystery, too...

MARCUS. And if there's time...figure out who stole the ice cream.

DAHLIA. Great. But first things first, Detective: what can I get you to drink? Now, I have coffee...

> *(Makes a dismissive face, then turns suddenly upbeat.)*

And I have tea!

MARCUS. Coffee, please.

DAHLIA. I should tell you, the tea leaves come from my garden.

MARCUS. Coffee's just fine.

DAHLIA. Well the coffee's over there.

MARCUS. I don't *need* a drink, Mrs. Whitney.

DAHLIA. *(Clearly upset.)* No, it's fine. You want coffee. No trouble at all. I'll get it.

> **(DAHLIA** *hobbles over to pour some coffee for* **MARCUS.)**

Excuse m'walking; I had a hip thing like a year ago.

MARCUS. That's fine.

DAHLIA. Well this is not how I imagined his birthday party going at all. Gunshots, detectives, everybody wanting coffee.

MARCUS. It was his birthday?

DAHLIA. Yeah – surprise!

MARCUS. Now we're getting somewhere. Mrs. Whitney, can you tell me exactly what happened tonight?

DAHLIA. Let's see. M'husband died. I had a hoagie. And then you showed up.

MARCUS. I don't think you understand. I need to know absolutely everything. Start a little further back and be as descriptive as possible.

[MUSIC NO. 05 "A PERFECTLY LOVELY SURPRISE"]

DAHLIA. M'story begins when I was a young, knock kneed scrap of a thing runnin' around Maycomb and throwing stones at the old Radley Place...

MARCUS. Okay. When I said "start further back" I didn't mean quite so far.

DAHLIA. Mrs. O'Callahan said, "You don't take off your top during class; that's not what young ladies do." Mrs. O'Callahan being m'college geometry professor...

MARCUS. When did your husband enter the picture?

DAHLIA. Ah! I was a young gal of eighteen or nineteen or thirty-five or such, and I was a dancer, as you can probably still see, despite m'hip issues, or as I call 'em, m'hip-shoes. Arthur was a big theater producer at the time. He saw me as I stepped off that bus in the big city and that's when our fairy tale romance began.

HE SAID I HAD A LOAD A' TALENTS
LIKE PERFECT PITCH
AND PERFECT BALANCE
AND EARS THAT WERE EQUAL IN SIZE
HE STICKS ME IN A COUPLE SHOWS AND M'STAR STARTS
    TO RISE
A PERFECTLY LOVELY SURPRISE

MARCUS. I see.

DAHLIA.

ONE NIGHT HE TOLD ME I WAS GRACEFUL

AND SAID I HAD A LOVELY FACE FULL
OF FEATURES LIKE EYEBROWS AND EYES
HIS HIGHFALUTIN WAY WITH WORDS SWEP' ME CLEAR
    OFF M'THIGHS
A PERFECTLY LOVELY SURPRISE

MARCUS. So he asked you to marry him?

DAHLIA.

YEAH BUT
LIKE EV'RYTHING IN LIFE
MEN ARE NEVER QUITE WHAT THEY SEEM
WE MARRIED IN THE FALL
THEN HE STOPPED M'WORK, BROKE M'HEART, KILLED
    M'DREAM

WHEN PROMISES OF FAME AND FOOTLIGHTS TURN OUT
    TO BE LIES
IT COMES AS A TOTAL SURPRISE

    (Through gritted teeth.)

A PERFECTLY LOVELY SURPRISE

MARCUS. You sound a little resentful of your husband, Mrs. Whitney.

DAHLIA. Me, resentful? Just 'cause he shoved me in the shadows the second we tied the knot? Maybe a skosh.

MARCUS. Then why did you throw him a surprise party?

DAHLIA. Because for years I've been plannin' to sing him a big show-stappin', toe-toppin' production number. Should I sing that one instead?

MARCUS. That's okay. You know, Mrs. Whitney, it sounds like this party wasn't for your husband at all.

DAHLIA. Why, Detective. You've got it all wrong.

I'VE ALWAYS TRIED TO BE A FUN WIFE
SO GUNNIN' T' BE NUMBER ONE WIFE...
Poor choice of words, I know.

I DID WHAT THAT TITLE IMPLIES
TO CELEBRATE HIS SPECIAL DAY, I BEGAN TO DEVISE
THIS PERFECTLY LOVELY SURPRISE

IT TOOK SOME TIME TO FORM THE GUEST LIST
WHICH BOILED DOWN TO JUST THE BEST LIST
OF FOLKS WHOM HE DIDN'T DESPISE

Including our niece Steph, who came up from the city.
Sweet gal, by the way.

I WENT AND BOUGHT A COUPLE CAKES WHICH I BAKED
INTO PIES
AND ALL FOR THIS LOVELY SURPRISE

MARCUS. And then?

DAHLIA.

WE FOUND A PLACE TO HIDE
THEN AT EIGHT O'CLOCK, IN HE CAME
WE YELLED "SURPRI –!" AND BANG
HE WAS ON THE FLOOR, DEAD AS DIRT... WHAT A SHAME

YA THINK YOU'LL ALWAYS HAVE A HUSBAND, THEN ONE
NIGHT HE DIES
A PERFECTLY LOVELY –

Did I say lovely? I meant awful.

AN AWFULLY PERFECT SURPRISE

MARCUS. Interesting story, Mrs. Whitney.

DAHLIA. Mm-hmm. And now for that song I meant to sing,
which goes a little something like –

MARCUS. Maybe later. I'd be a pretty sorry excuse for a
detective if I didn't hear from everyone in the room
first. Uh... Dr. Griff! You're a familiar face. Did you see
anything tonight?

> (**THE SUSPECTS** *becomes* **DR. GRIFF**, *a gruff but
> friendly psychiatrist.*)

DR. GRIFF. Well, yes, I did. I saw a patient finally achieve
his dream of becoming a detective. Congratulations,
you! I haven't been this proud since you finally started
dealing with your crippling depression after discovering
the true, dark nature of your partner slash lover.

MARCUS. Dr. Griff! I think you're violating doctor-patient
confidentiality.

DR. GRIFF. Schmoctor-schmatient schmonfidentiality. We're all friends.

>   *(Suddenly serious.)*

We are friends, aren't we, Marcus?

MARCUS. Well, sure, Dr. Griff.

DR. GRIFF. Close friends?

MARCUS. I don't know. I guess.

DR. GRIFF. Close enough to sing a song about friendship?

MARCUS. Let's move on.

>   **(THE SUSPECTS** *becomes* **BARRETTE LEWIS,** *an elegant, poised, overdramatic ballerina.)*

MARCUS. I don't suppose you know anything about the murder, miss?

BARRETTE. Whose murder?

MARCUS. Mr. Whitney's.

BARRETTE. You're so sure it was murder?

MARCUS. He was shot in the forehead.

BARRETTE. Oh. Well, then...whodunit?

MARCUS. That's what we're here to find out, Miss Lewis.

BARRETTE. Oh! You know me.

MARCUS. *(Shyly.)* I've seen you dance many times, Miss Lewis. In fact, this is the first time I've seen you not dancing. You're good at that too.

BARRETTE. *(Flirtatiously.)* Why, thank you...young man.

>   *(She gets incredibly close to* **MARCUS** *and touches his face.)*

MARCUS. *(Nervously.)* Uh, Miss Lewis, I should probably ask you some questions.

BARRETTE. I must say I have great respect for you boys in blue.

[MUSIC NO. 06 "SO..."]

MARCUS.

>   SO BEAUTIFUL

BARRETTE. Why, every time I've had a run-in with the fuzz, I've been surprised by how kind they were...and how trusting.

MARCUS.

SO ELEGANT

BARRETTE. I only wish I didn't cross their paths quite so frequently...and under such...dreadful circumstances.

MARCUS.

SO INNOCENT

BARRETTE.

SO...

MARCUS.

SO –

> *(*THE SUSPECTS *becomes* STEPH WHITNEY, *an overeager grad student.)*

STEPH. Hey Detective, do you mind if I pipe in for a sec?

MARCUS. Excuse me, who are you?

STEPH. I'm Steph Whitney, Arthur and Dahlia's niece.

MARCUS. Oh?

DAHLIA. This is our niece, Steph. She came up from the city. Sweet gal.

MARCUS. Oh.

STEPH. Yeah, this is just such a coincidence. I don't know if you knew but I'm getting my masters in criminology and, strangely enough, writing my thesis, which is called...guess what.

MARCUS. I don't –

STEPH. *How to Assist in the Solving of a Small-Town Murder*!

MARCUS. That's the name of your *thesis*?

STEPH. Yeah, and until now I was really drawing a blank. I'm so sad my uncle's dead, of course, but in terms of my career in academia...

MARCUS. Good luck with that, Miss Whitney.

STEPH. But there is one problem.

MARCUS. Yes, Miss Whitney?

STEPH. Call me Steph. It seems to me that the most effective crime-solving partners throughout history were so in sync with each other, that in a moment of absolute peril, one of them could yell something like "cocktail umbrella," and the other one...

> (*Mimes elbowing a bad guy.*)

...would just instinctively know what to do.

MARCUS. "Cocktail umbrella"? I'm not following.

STEPH. It's just...we're obviously not that close yet, but if I'm gonna help –

MARCUS. Whoa. Steph. You're not gonna help. I let someone help me once before, and let's just say it didn't...help.

DR. GRIFF. He's referring to when he discovered the true, dark nature of his partner slash lover slash –

MARCUS. Let's just say it didn't help!

STEPH. I assume, then, that you're about to ask us all to reenact the exact moment of the crime, and surely you'll need a hand wrangling the masses...

MARCUS. Thanks but no thanks. Reenacting the exact moment of the crime is actually the *last* step according to protocol. First we – and by we I mean I – question each of the suspects and evaluate possible motives.

[MUSIC NO. 07 "MURRAY & BARB CUE"]

> (**THE SUSPECTS** *changes to* **MURRAY** *and* **BARB**, *a squabbling middle-aged couple.*)

MURRAY. I know who did it!

BARB. Murray!

MURRAY. Quiet, Barb. Yes, I may be able to shed some light on the matter, Detective.

BARB. Murray, I'm warning you...

MARCUS. And you two are?

MURRAY. Murray Flandon. And my wife, Barb. You know, the feisty old couple you saw through that window.

MARCUS. Uh, right. And your connection to Arthur Whitney?

MURRAY. We've been his neighbors for nearly twenty years.

BARB. And I used to cut Mr. Whitney's hair.

MARCUS. I'm sure you did a fine job. Kinda hard to tell now, with part of his head missing. Anyway, I'd greatly appreciate any pertinent information you may have.

[MUSIC NO. 08 "IT WAS HER"]

MURRAY. Of course. My conscience compels me to speak, despite the fact that certain...pressures have tried their best to keep me silent.

BARB.
      MURRAY, I SWEAR TO GOD...

MURRAY.
      I CANNOT HIDE THE TRUTH
      I'VE GOT THE ANSWER

BARB.
      MURRAY!

MURRAY.
      YOU MIGHT AS WELL RELAX
      FOR I'M CONFIDENT THE FACTS CONCUR

BARB.
      SHUT IT!

MURRAY.
      I'VE HAD IT FIGURED OUT
      SINCE IT BEGAN, SIR

BARB.
      ASS!

MURRAY.
      I KNOW BEYOND A DOUBT...

BARB. Murray, don't!

MURRAY.
      IT WAS HER!

MARCUS. Your wife?

MURRAY. Yes. *J'accuse.*

BARB. This is the third time you've accused me of homicide this month.

MURRAY. This time I'm sure.

BARB. Stop accusing me, Murray!

MURRAY. Stop killing people, *Baaaaarb*!

MARCUS. Your wife seems to think you do this pretty often, Mr. Flandon.

MURRAY. She would say that. But consider this:

>THERE'S NOTHING BUT LIES
>UNDERNEATH THOSE EYES
>THEY SEEM COLLECTED AND COOL
>BUT DON'T LET 'EM FOOL YOU
>
>THE MINUTE BLOOD WAS SPILT

MARCUS. What exactly happened?

MURRAY.

>I TOOK A WHIFF, SIR

>>*(Sniffs* **BARB** *and reels.)*

>THE WOMAN REEKED OF GUILT

MARCUS. But the killer...

MURRAY.

>IT WAS HER!

MARCUS. What possible motive could she have had, Murray?

MURRAY. Enough, Detective. You've heard the facts, now arrest that woman!

BARB. Don't let Murray bully you around, Detective. You know, I don't even know how I wound up with that louse.

MARCUS. Why don't you two take it easy?

BARB.

>HAD
>MY PICK OF GUYS
>WHY HIM?

MURRAY. Why indeed.

BARB.
 HE'S CONSTANTLY CRUEL

MARCUS. Let's not make this personal, folks.

BARB.
 AND GET A LOAD A' HOW HE'S BUILT

MURRAY. Watch it, you!

BARB.
 HE'S SO STIFF

MURRAY. Like your mother!

BARB.
 DON'T SAY IT!

MARCUS. As much as I wish I could offer some sort of couples counseling, protocol says stick to the facts.

BARB. *(To* **MURRAY.***)* You've never been able to handle the *fact* that I got class.

MURRAY. I wouldn't call Weight Watchers a class, more of a program.

BARB. At least I don't have a small penis!

MURRAY. You might. We won't know till you reach your goal weight!

 (Beat.)

 THERE'S NOTHING

BARB.
 HAD

MURRAY.
 BUT LIES

BARB.
 MY PICK OF GUYS

MURRAY.
 UNDERNEATH THOSE EYES

BARB.
 WHY HIM?

MURRAY.
 THEY SEEM COLLECTED AND COOL

BARB.
>   HE'S CONSTANTLY CRUEL

MURRAY.
>   BUT DON'T LET 'EM FOOL YOU
>   THE MINUTE BLOOD WAS SPILT

BARB.
>   GET A LOAD A' HOW HE'S BUILT

MURRAY.
>   I TOOK A WHIFF, SIR

BARB.
>   HE'S SO STIFF

MURRAY.
>   THE WOMAN REEKED OF GUILT

BARB.
>   DON'T SAY IT!

MURRAY.
>   IT WAS –

BARB. Don't say it, you son of a bitch!

>   (**MURRAY** *opens his mouth to speak.*)

Murray! I'm warning you!

>   (*Beat, then lustfully.*)

You tough man.

>   (**MURRAY** *and* **BARB** *begin making out furiously.* **MARCUS** *bangs on the piano to get their attention.*)

MARCUS. Hey. *Hey!* God, you two are acting just like –

>   (*Light bulb.*)

[MUSIC NO. 09 "THE MOTIVE (UNDERSCORE)"]

MARCUS. Aha! Okay, everybody, we're back. And I've got the motive.

STEPH. But you hardly know anything about us.

MARCUS. I know a lot more about you than you think. For example: Steph! I know that you drove your kindergarten teacher to drink by asking too many questions.

STEPH. Oh my God.

MARCUS. And Barb! You only became a hair stylist so you could spend your life maliciously spreading gossip.

BARB. What a load!

MARCUS. And Mrs. Whitney! I know you cheated in a pie-baking contest.

DAHLIA. Hey! The only time in my life that I ever cheated was in a pie-baking...oh, right.

MARCUS. I can't believe I didn't see it before.

STEPH. What are you getting at?

MARCUS. Listening to that feisty old couple, I was suddenly reminded of an early Arthur Whitney novel...

MARCUS & STEPH. *The Feisty Old Couple*!

(Without meaning to, they touch hands excitedly. They catch themselves and pull away.)

MARCUS. That's when it all came together. Over the years, Whitney used each and every one of you as characters in his books. And those stories were only partly fictional, weren't they? They all contained at least one dirty little secret. Possibly enough to make one of you seek revenge.

MURRAY. That's preposterous. The man in *The Feisty Old Couple* actually loves his wife.

MARCUS. *Your* dirty little secret, Murray. I wondered why a successful novelist only had a handful of people at his birthday party. Everybody hated him!

BARB. Of course we hated him.

MARCUS. So we all have a motive!

STEPH. What was that?

MARCUS. I said you all have a motive.

STEPH. No, you said, "*We* all have a –"

MARCUS. No I didn't.

STEPH. Yes you did.

MARCUS. No, I didn't.

STEPH. Oh my God. Am I crazy, you guys? Dr. Griff, you heard him, right?

DR. GRIFF. Yes, and in my profession, that's what's known as a Freudian sex.

MARCUS. Don't be ridiculous, Steph. Lou and I can't be suspects because we've never been characters in Arthur Whitney novels.

STEPH. Well, maybe Lou hasn't, but you were!

MARCUS. What?

STEPH. Marcus Moscowicz? I knew that name sounded familiar! Haven't you ever read *Unsolved Hearts*?

MARCUS. Guess I missed it. Anyway –

> (**STEPH** *picks up one of the several books scattered on the floor.*)

STEPH. Look, there's a description on the back. A tale of crippling depression unfolds as Jarcus Joscowicz vows to never love again after discovering the true, dark nature of his beautiful partner slash lover slash slag slash seductress slash – *(To the room.)* This is like a tongue-twister, you guys! Slash –

MARCUS. That's quite enough, Steph! That book has nothing to do with me!

DAHLIA. Careful, everybody. He's acting like he did in the book.

MARCUS. I'm not acting like I did in the book!

DAHLIA. He said, "I'm not acting like I did in the book" in the book!

MARCUS. No I –!

> *(Composes himself.)*

That character could've been based on any cop in New England. Maybe it's based on Lou!

DAHLIA. I'm gonna go ahead and nip this one in the butt. None of my stupid husband's stupid books is about stupid Lou.

MARCUS. How can you be so certain?

DAHLIA. Because I remember what he said to me the day he started writing *Unsolved Hearts*. He said, and I'm quoting now, "I just got three ideas: one, to write a detective romance based on the life of someone named Marcus and not Lou. Two, to never write a book about Lou. Three, cheeseburgers for dinner – you down?"

MARCUS. You make it sound like he knew everything about everybody in town. How is that possible?

STEPH. That's what we're here to find out, Detective.

MARCUS. Stop saying "we"!

STEPH. I mean the royal "we," like you and me, together, as a team.

MARCUS. That's the same – good lord, Steph! I don't have all night! I've managed to find the motive but that still leaves step two according to protocol: discover to whom the motive most applies.

DR. GRIFF. Excuse me, Marcus, but all this talk about motives started me in wondering if you ever read a little Arthur Whitney gem called *The Friendly Old Psychiatrist is Innocent*.

MARCUS. Yeah. Are you suggesting that book was about –

DR. GRIFF. Yep, guilty. I mean, innocent!

MARCUS. Well then, Doctor, it seems you're momentarily off the hook.

DR. GRIFF. Now, Marcus, I don't want any special treatment just because we got that best friend bike ride tomorrow.

MARCUS. I don't remember saying I could do that.

DR. GRIFF. *(Deadly serious.)* I don't remember asking.

    (Back to smiling.)

Now was someone peddling tea before?

MARCUS. Tea?

DAHLIA. He wants tea? Oh it's no trouble. I'll get it!

MARCUS. You made her day, Doctor. Seems like nobody else is having any.

MARCUS & STEPH. *(Beat.)* Hmm...

MARCUS. Only one drinking tea...

STEPH. And the subject of my uncle's only flattering exposé. Someone sticks out like a sore thumb. Or should I say "thumb-one." Let's grill him, Detective.

MARCUS. Is that what *you* would do next, Steph?

STEPH. Oh, definitely. Or should I say... "stephinitely."

MARCUS. Well, unfortunately you're wrong once again. If I'm going to compare and contrast the weight of your various dirty little secrets, I need to find out exactly what Whitney exposed about each and every one of you. And to be perfectly honest, I'm not entirely sure which book detailed the life of Miss Lewis. Which leaves only one possible course of action: fix my hair and begin a strictly professional interrogation of...

> *(Turns.)*

Miss Lewis.

(Shyly.) Hi.

> *(Back to business.)*

Exactly what did Mr. Whitney write about you and who else knows about it? Your...boyfriend?

STEPH. Okay, grilling time's over! Let's recap, you and me, go. Okay, so: we all have a motive because of my uncle's stories.

MARCUS. Well –

STEPH. So how well do we know my uncle's stories?

MARCUS. Very well.

STEPH. Good, because I practically have them memorized, I love them so much. I even like his story *My Niece is a Dumb Grad Student Who Asks Too Many Questions.*

MARCUS. I know all the man's stories. Except that *Unsolved Hearts* thing...you...

> *(Beat.)*

Miss Lewis.

STEPH. Still me.

MARCUS. Well, I want to talk to Miss Lewis.

STEPH. Well, she's busy.

MARCUS. She was just sitting there, drinking coffee.

STEPH. She probably still is. But the point, Detective, is that we need to rehash every one of his stories.

MARCUS. *(Placating her.)* Okay. We will. You and me. Every story. But later, Steph, okay? Later. Now, Miss Lewis.

STEPH. *(Long beat.)* Still me.

(**MARCUS** *sighs.*)

I'm sorry, it's just kind of funny that you want to interview Barrette Lewis before you've even met everyone that's in the room. I mean, you haven't even acknowledged the twelve-member boys choir in the corner.

MARCUS. *(Thrown.)* Twelve-member...? One moment, Miss Lewis.

(Composing himself.)

Hi boys, we have to get you out of here. Protocol says remove all minors from the scene of the crime.

(**THE SUSPECTS** *becomes* **TIMMY**, *the choir's wiseacre*, Little Rascals-*esque spokesman.)

TIMMY. Aw, don't worry about us, Chief. I'm nine.

MARCUS. Well, adorable as that may be, this is no place for innocent eyes. I can't imagine why you're even here tonight.

TIMMY. We was hired what for to be the entertainment. The name's Timmy. And that's Yonkers...

(**THE SUSPECTS** *waves hello as* **YONKERS**.)

And that's Skid!

(**THE SUSPECTS** *waves as* **SKID**. **MARCUS** *takes a moment to acknowledge* **TIMMY**'s *antiquated style of speech.*)

MARCUS. Where are you from?

TIMMY. We's from Badoinkaville.

MARCUS. Oh, Badoinkaville. I should've recognized the accent.

TIMMY. Yeah…

MARCUS. Well, I'm sure this must be pretty difficult for you youngsters.

[MUSIC NO. 10 "A LOT WOISE"]

TIMMY. Difficult? Cause a' one lousy dead body? You got a lot to loin about kids, Chief.

WE BEEN AROUND THE BLOCK A TIME OR TWO AND SEEN
  A LOT ALL RIGHT
DON'T IMAGINE THAT WE'RE NOT ALL RIGHT
'CAUSE WE SEEN A LOT WOISE

TO TELL THE TRUTH IF WE WAS YOUNGER, WE'D BE
  GETTIN' SICKER NOW
BUT OUR SKIN'S A LITTLE THICKER NOW
'CAUSE WE SEEN A LOT WOISE

WE SEEN A FELLA TORN IN TWO ONE DAY
BY A GORILLA AT THE ZOO ONE DAY
WE HARDLY EVER MAKE IT THROUGH ONE DAY
WITHOUT A GLIMPSE OF HORROR
NO NEED TO INTERVENE, WE SEEN A LOT WOISE

MARCUS. I remember what it felt like to be your age, Timmy. Trying to be brave. Wanting to impress the crowd. It's okay if you're scared.

TIMMY. Scared? Over this? This ain't nothin'!

MARCUS. Says you.

TIMMY. Says me in a big way, brother! Go ahead, Yonkers, tell 'im what I mean.

YONKERS.

YOU NEEDN'T BOTHER THINKIN' STUFF LIKE THIS COULD
  BE DEPRAVIN' US
IT'S A LITTLE LATE FOR SAVIN' US
'CAUSE WE SEEN A LOT WOISE

MARCUS. Well…

YONKERS.

> WE SEEN A CHUMP WHO HELD HIS BREATH FOR LONGER
>> THAN AN HOUR ONCE
> SAW MY GRANNY IN THE SHOWER ONCE
> YEAH, WE SEEN A LOT WOISE!

TIMMY.

> WE SEEN A BABY BEIN' BORN ONE DAY
> WE SEEN A FAT GUY EATIN' CORN ONE DAY
> WE SEEN 'EM BOTH WHILE WATCHIN' PORN ONE DAY
> AND STILL WE GO ON SMILIN'
> BRUDDER, IT'S ALL ROUTINE, WE SEEN A LOT WOISE

MARCUS. Uh-huh. There's a number I want you boys to call when you get home.

TIMMY. Say, you're okay, Chief! I tells ya what: you ever need anything, you just whistle. You know how to whistle, don't you? Show 'im, Yonkers!

YONKERS. *(Strangely sensuous.)* You just…put your lips togedda…and…

MARCUS. Yes, Yonkers! I know how to whistle.

TIMMY. Well, you just whistle and the whole choir's got your back, any place, any time!

MARCUS. By the way, how come your twelve-member boys choir only consists of you three boys?

TIMMY. Oh, that's a funny story that also happens to fit poifectly unto our refrain. Tell 'im, Skid!

SKID.

> WENT ON A CAMPING TRIP AND LOST NINE MEMBERS OF
>> THE CHOIR THERE
> WHEN OUR TENT WAS SET ON FIRE THERE
> YEAH, WE SEEN A LOT WOISE

MARCUS. I'm so sorry.

SKID.

> I CAN'T IMAGINE HOW MY BEST PAL JOHNNY MUSTA FELT
>> THAT NIGHT
> WHEN HIS FACE BEGAN TO MELT THAT NIGHT
> BOY, WE SEEN A LOT WOISE

TIMMY.

> WE SPENT A NIGHT TRAPPED IN IKEA ONCE
> BESIDE A KID WITH DIARRHEA ONCE
> WE SAW A SHOW CALLED *MAMMA MIA!* ONCE
> AND STILL WE'RE SOMEHOW SMILIN'!

YONKERS.

> DANCE BREAK!

TIMMY. Charleston! Time step! Wings!

SKID.

> NO SIR, WE AIN'T PRISTINE, WE SEEN A LOT –

YONKERS.

> STUFF WHAT COULD TURN YA GREEN, WE SEEN A LOT –

TIMMY.

> AND IF WE REACH THIRTEEN, WE'LL SEE A LOT WOISE!

MARCUS. Fine, you can stay. But if anyone else dies, you're going straight outside.

TIMMY. *(Darkly.)* Yes, it soitenly would be tragical if someone else was to get whacked.

MARCUS. What's that, Timmy?

TIMMY. Quick, Yonkers, hit him with our catchphrase!

YONKERS. Aww, bananas.

MARCUS. *(Utterly charmed.)* "Bananas," that's so cute! Bananas.

[MUSIC NO. 11 "BANANAS / NEXT BOOK CUE"]

(Light bulb.)

Bananas! *All of Them Bananas*! Of course! Everyone has a motive, but it stands to reason that the person with the most motive is whoever would've had the most to lose if Arthur Whitney had been able to finish his latest novel, *All of Them Bananas*. In other words, ladies and gentlemen, whom was his next book going to be about?

*(**YONKERS** plays the expected dramatic chords.)*

Thank you.

YONKERS. You're welcome.

MARCUS. Now, Mrs. Whitney. Did your husband tell you anything about his next book?

DAHLIA. Mr. Megaphone used to blah blah blah about *All of Them Bananas* day and night.

MARCUS. That's fantastic!

DAHLIA. But I actually have the ability to close my ears, and that's what I did every time he mentioned the title.

MARCUS. Close your ears?

DAHLIA. You want a demonstration?

MARCUS. No.

DAHLIA. Talk.

MARCUS.	**DAHLIA.**
That's okay, Mrs. Whitney. I really don't – Mrs. Whitney – stop it, Mrs. Whitney!	What? What's that? I can't hear him. Really, everybody, I can't hear a thing!

       (Beat.)

DAHLIA. Amazing, i'n'it?

MARCUS. So you have no clue whom the book was going to be about?

DAHLIA. I'm afraid to answer that question, Detective, you'd have to do one of two things: talk to a dead man...or look in his notebook.

MARCUS. There's a notebook?

DAHLIA. Yeah, upstairs next to the bed.

       (Holds up her hand.)

It looks just like my hand, except it's a book.

MARCUS. All right, Lou, watch them for a second. I'll be right back with that book, and hopefully the name of our killer!

       (He runs offstage.)

DAHLIA. Since he's finally gone, let's have me sing you that big song I might have mentioned earlier.

(DAHLIA *opens her mouth to sing just as* MARCUS *runs back into the room.)*

MARCUS. It's gone!

DAHLIA. Gone? Why, that's impossible!

MARCUS. I can only assume the notebook was stolen, but short of doing a strip search, there's nothing I can do but continue the interrogation.

(At *"strip search,"* DAHLIA *begins undressing. She gets two buttons undone when* MARCUS *catches her eye and shakes his head "no." She turns forward and undoes one more button.)*

No!

(She stops.)

Now, Miss Lewis, I believe I'm still waiting for a straight answer about your literary connection to Arthur Whitney. Can you bring me up to speed?

DR. GRIFF. Why are you asking me?

MARCUS. I'm not.

DR. GRIFF. Doesn't matter. As long as I've got your attention, there's something I should tell you. Now buddy, I normally wouldn't do this, because it's about one of my...

(Winks.)

Schmatients. But considering we're like brothers, I do have some information you might want to write down.

MARCUS. Fine. Lou, write this down.

(To DR. GRIFF.*)* You were saying?

DR. GRIFF. Not here! Too crowded. Better have a secret best friend meeting outside in five minutes.

(MARCUS *starts to walk away.)*

Wait! To seal the deal, maybe we should do our secret handshake.

MARCUS. We don't have a –

(DR. GRIFF *awkwardly jabs at* MARCUS*'s hands.)*

Oh. Okay. Yes. Ha ha. Very good. Thank you, Doctor. But once and for all I really need to finish –

>(**MARCUS**'s *cell phone rings.* **DAHLIA**, *thinking the sound came from the audience, steps downstage.*)

DAHLIA. (*Enraged.*) What was that? Turn 'em off.

MARCUS. (*Steps aside to answer his phone.*) Hey! Yep, everything's fine, Chief. Detective Grayson will be here in thirty minutes? Okay...okay...bye.

>(*Hangs up.*)

Thirty minutes, Lou.

>(**MARCUS** *shudders and returns to the room.*)

Where was I?

STEPH. Examining facts?

MARCUS. No.

STEPH. Searching for clues?

MARCUS. No!

STEPH. Noticing that I reapplied my lip gloss?

MARCUS. No! Steph! I won't be ready to do any of that until I've settled things with Vanessa.

STEPH. Vanessa?

MARCUS. I mean Miss Lewis.

>(*Turns.*)

Now, then, Miss Lewis: how much does your boyfriend know and does he exist?

BARRETTE. (*Jumps.*) Now you see what you've made me do, Detective? You've made me spill my coffee. My leotard is hot and wet. Soon it will be cold and wet. That won't do. I have to change.

MARCUS. You can't leave, Miss Lewis.

BARRETTE. It's all right. I brought six leotards and have only gone through four. And the party's almost over, so...

MARCUS. Fine, Miss Lewis, you can change. But I have to watch you. By which I mean...be with you. Not *with* you, of course; there's bound to be some sort of solid, professional door between us, obviously, because protocol...would you excuse me one minute? Lou!

(MARCUS takes LOU aside.)

I'm not sure what to do, Lou. That woman is clearly falling in love with me.

(Beat.)

You're right. I won't be able to focus until I get her alone and establish some boundaries.

(MARCUS steps back to face the room.)

Now, Miss Lewis, you go change behind this curtain.

(Leads her off.)

And when Miss Lewis gets done I'm going to want to talk to her alone.

STEPH. That's good technique.

MARCUS. Yes, good. Would everyone mind leaving?

STEPH. Wait, me too?

MARCUS. You first and foremost, Steph. Lou, keep an eye on them.

DAHLIA. C'mon, everybody, let's take off our shoes and go slide around in the kitchen.

MARCUS. That's the spirit, Mrs. Whitney. Thank you!

(STEPH starts to leave with the crowd, but instead crosses back to MARCUS.)

STEPH. Detective, I think it's really helpful to have a second point of view when you're conducting this sort of –

MARCUS. *(Ushering her out of the room.)* Steph, I'm not going to listen to another word out of you until you're on the other side of that door.

STEPH. But then you won't be able to hear me.

MARCUS. Exactly!

(MARCUS slams the door in her face. He stops, reconsiders, and opens the door again.)

Listen. Maybe after I wrap this up we can talk about your thesis. Can you hang tight?

STEPH. Yeah! I'll just go grab a...

(Winks.)

"Cocktail umbrella," if you know what I –

MARCUS. Sounds good!

(He slams the door again.)

STEPH. – mean. How do you work with that guy, Lou? Does he always ask people questions without giving them a chance to respond?

(Barreling on.)

God, it's so annoying when people do that, don't you think?

(Barreling on again.)

Me too.

[MUSIC NO. 12 "HE NEEDS A PARTNER"]

(Beat.)

No, I'm not saying he's a bad detective. *Au contraire.* He's nearly perfect the way he is.

(Beat.)

Nearly.

HE DOESN'T NEED A LOT
HE'S DOING ALMOST FINE
WITH THE SKILLS THAT HE'S GOT
I COULDN'T NAME A THING
HE'S WITHOUT
...JUST ABOUT
HE'S PRACTIC'LY COMPLETE AS CAN BE
EXCEPT HE DOESN'T HAVE...
NEVER MIND

HE'S REALLY HALFWAY THERE
HE KNOWS A LOT OF RULES
IN FACT, MORE THAN HIS SHARE

HE'S TOTALLY EQUIPPED
FOR SUCCESS
...I MEAN, MORE OR LESS
HIS HEAD IS OVERFLOWING WITH FACTS
BUT STILL THERE'S ONE THING HE LACKS
I THINK HE NEEDS A PARTNER
SOME KIND OF PARTNER
A YOUNG, VIVACIOUS PARTNER
NO, NOT LIKE YOU, LOU, THOUGH I'M SURE YOU'RE VERY
    GOOD AT WHAT YOU DO
BUT YOU SEE
HE NEEDS A PARTNER LIKE...

MARCUS. Let me know if you need anything, Barrette. A hand with one of those hard-to-reach zippers, perhaps, or...anything at all.

(*To himself.*) Easy, Marcus, easy. She may be beautiful, but don't forget... Vanessa was beautiful too.

> (**THE SUSPECTS** *pantomimes the actions of the following.*)

Sure, she was beautiful all right. But it would be a stretch to say she followed all the rules of being a police officer. It started out innocently enough. At first the chief only caught her doing small things like forgetting to file paperwork. Pretty soon it was bigger things. Like chopping up her friends and family. The chief called her into his office to confront her about the killings. He said, "Vanessa, I hate to tell you this, but we've got your fingerprints all over the bodies." And Vanessa said, "For a dollar fifty more you could have me all over *your* body, too." Then the chief said, "Three eye witnesses saw you do it." And Vanessa said, "Three eyes, huh? I met a man in [*name of local town*] with three legs – how do you like that one, kids?" And the chief said, "Vanessa, nothing you're saying is making sense." And Vanessa said, "And a how-de-doo to you too, buckaroo." But as she turned to go...

> (**VANESSA** *picks up her briefcase and turns to go, but when she does, it opens and a*

*collection of realistic-looking body parts
spills out. Beat.)*

(As **VANESSA**.*)* "Ya think that's bad, you should see the other guy."

(Beat.)

I told Vanessa I would wait for her while she paid her debt to society, but she hung herself in prison. Right before she died, she uttered these haunting last words...

(As **VANESSA**.*)* "You know something? A hung woman isn't nearly as much fun as a hung ma –"

(Cut off by a strangulation noise.)

After that, all I could do was drown my misery in a pool of alcohol, books on protocol, and, of course, the piano lessons. That's when I vowed to never love again.

BARRETTE. I'll be out in a minute.

MARCUS.

BUT I'M ALL THROUGH
   WITH TEARS
IT'S FUNNY HOW THE PAIN
OVER TIME, DISAPPEARS
THERE'S SO MUCH MORE
   TO LIFE
I WON'T KNOW
UNLESS I LET GO
I HAVE TO LEARN TO
   TRUST SOMEONE NEW
AND NOW I THINK I KNOW
   WHO

STEPH.

I THINK HE NEEDS A PARTNER

SOME KIND OF PARTNER

BARRETTE MIGHT BE THE ONE

TAKE OUT MY HEART, IT'S DONE

A YOUNG AND PEPPY PARTNER

I SEE NOW

MARCUS.	STEPH.
HOW NO	I'M SURE A LOT OF GIRLS
ONE ELSE	ARE QUALIFIED BUT
	NONE OF THEM
WILL DO	WILL DO

STEPH.

'CAUSE YOU SEE
HE NEEDS A PARTNER LIKE...
HE NEEDS A PARTNER LIKE...
HE NEEDS A PARTNER...
PERIOD.

> *(Beat.)*

You know, I'm glad you're here, Lou. If it weren't for you, I'd just be thinking all these things.

> **(THE SUSPECTS** *exits as* **STEPH** *and reenters as* **BARRETTE** *from behind the curtain.)*

BARRETTE. Oh, they've gone!

MARCUS. I know.

BARRETTE. Okay, just making sure.

MARCUS. Miss Lewis –

BARRETTE. Why can't you leave me alone?

MARCUS. Well, I can't. This is an investigation.

BARRETTE. And this is a *ronde de jambe*.

> *(She does one.)*

MARCUS. Let me talk to you.

BARRETTE. Let me *ronde de jambe*!

MARCUS. Stop! Have a seat, Miss Lewis!

> *(He forcibly sits her down at the piano.)*

And relax.

MARCUS. *(Indicating the keyboard.)* Rest your hands here, if that's more comfortable.

> *(She does as he says.)*

[MUSIC NO. 13 "SO WHAT IF I DID?"]

BARRETTE. You do enjoy accusing people, don't you?

MARCUS.
>SO BEAUTIFUL

BARRETTE. Well, I've decided I'm not afraid of you anymore. And I have nothing to conceal.

MARCUS.
>SO ELEGANT

BARRETTE. After all, who cares how close I was to the victim?

MARCUS.
>SO INNO —
>WHAT?

BARRETTE.
>SO WHAT IF I KNEW HIM QUITE WELL
>MUCH BETTER THAN MOST MIGHT HAVE KNOWN?
>HE LOVED ME, THEN LEFT
>HIS BARRETTE WAS BEREFT
>BUT THAT'S NOT A LEAD
>SO LEAVE ME ALONE

MARCUS. You were lovers?

BARRETTE.
>SO WHAT IF I STOLE ALL HIS PICTURES
>AND VI'LENTLY SCRATCHED OUT HIS FACE?
>I MAY SEEM ALOOF
>BUT THAT'S A TRAIT, NOT PROOF
>SO TRUST ME, YOU HAVEN'T A CASE

MARCUS. Well, I'm sure you're probably innocent, but still...

BARRETTE.
>SO WHAT IF THIS MORNING WE GOT IN A FIGHT?
>SO WHAT?
>WHO CARES WHAT WE SAID?
>SO WHAT IF I TOLD HIM I'D KILL HIM TONIGHT?
>WELL, THAT'S WHAT ONE SAYS WHEN ONE WANTS
>>SOMEONE DEAD
>
>SO WHAT IF HIS DEATH MAKES ME GIGGLE
>
>>*(Giggles.)*
>
>AND BLITHE AS SOME ROPE-SKIPPING KID?
>I MAY SEEM A NUT

BUT IF I AM, SO WHAT?
THOUGH NIGHTS I UNCLOTHED HIM
WHEN DAWN BROKE, I LOATHED HIM
SO FIERCELY, SO WHAT IF I DID?

MARCUS. Then again, you do have the right to remain silent if you'd rather wait –

BARRETTE.

SO WHAT IF I'M HOLDING A GUN?

*(She holds one up; **MARCUS** takes a step back.)*

A GUN THAT I RECENTLY BOUGHT
IT'S MISSING A ROUND
WHICH I'M SURE WILL BE FOUND
BUT THAT DOESN'T PROVE
THAT ARTHUR WAS SHOT

MARCUS. He *was* shot, Barrette.

BARRETTE.

AND WHAT OF MY CRIMINAL RECORD?
SO WHAT IF I'VE KILLED A FEW MEN?
I ONCE WAS DERANGED

(Gives deranged look.)

BUT AS YOU SEE, I'VE CHANGED
SO WHY WOULD I TRY IT AGAIN?

MARCUS. Killed a few men?

BARRETTE. It was self-defense...and that entire jury of young, persuadable men agreed.

MARCUS. *(Grim.)* I think I understand, Barrette.

BARRETTE.

SO WHAT IF I'M JUMPY AND SKITTISH AND TENSE?
SO WHAT?
WE ALL HAVE OUR FLAWS
SO WHAT IF MY SENTENCES END IN...

(Long beat.)

...SUSPENSE!
WELL, THAT'S HOW ONE TALKS WHEN ONE'S GRASPING
    AT STRAWS
SO WHAT IF I SPENT ALL OF SUNDAY

MALICIOUSLY FORGING HIS WILL?
I LEFT ME A LOT
WELL IF I DID, SO WHHHHAT?
THOUGH BLOOD IS UNSIGHTLY
I'VE DREAMT OF IT NIGHTLY
SO WHAT IF I, WHAT IF I,
WHAT IF I...

> (**BARRETTE** *breaks into a violent dream ballet, which develops into* **THE SUSPECTS** *and* **MARCUS** *performing a four-handed boogie-woogie on the piano. When they're ready to get back to the show,* **THE SUSPECTS** *again becomes* **BARRETTE***, who holds up her hand as* **ARTHUR***'s notebook.)*

THOUGH THEFT ISN'T WHOLESOME
I STEALTHILY STOLE SOME-
THING YOU LEFT TO LOOK FOR
THAT INFAMOUS BOOK FOR
WHICH ARTHUR HAD GOTTEN
TO JOT DOWN HIS PLOT IN
SO WHAT IF I, WHAT IF I, WHAT IF I –

> *(Inhales.)*

WHAT IF I, WHAT IF I –
DID...
I say stole? I meant...it was a present!
SO WHAT?

MARCUS. That's Arthur Whitney's book of notes! Where'd you get that?

BARRETTE. I told you...it was a present. Marcus, you shouldn't have.

MARCUS. I didn't! Miss Lewis, you're lying and everyone knows it!

BARRETTE. Who's everyone?

MARCUS. *(Gestures around the room.)* Everyone!

BARRETTE. Oh, when did they get back?

MARCUS. A good five minutes ago.

MURRAY. We got bored.

MARCUS. Miss Lewis, you stole that. I can't believe I almost thought we could share a life together.

STEPH. I see. Excuse me, I have a reprise to sing offstage.

(*She leaves.*)

MARCUS. Miss Lewis, about that –

STEPH. (*Offstage, a capella.*)

I THOUGHT HE NEEDED A PARTNER

MARCUS. About that notebook.

DAHLIA. You hussy! I heard what she said; she said she was...*fermiliar* with my husband! I thought so, especially those nights when she joined us in bed. But this confirms it!

MARCUS. Mrs. Whitney, please.

DAHLIA. I'm so mad, I could just stop the show with my big song.

(*Catching* **MARCUS**'s *eye.*)

No? Even now? Fine.

MARCUS. Start talking, Barrette.

BARRETTE. All right! I stole it. I was sure that his next book would have revealed our indiscretion. I didn't want a scandal, so I –

MARCUS. Stole the notebook.

BARRETTE. Yes. Please don't be angry with me, Detective Marcus, everybody, Lou. I stole the notebook but I didn't kill him.

(*Cozying up to* **MARCUS**.)

You believe me, don't you?

MARCUS. Not this time, lady! Hand over the –

(**MARCUS**'s *cell phone rings again. As before,* **DAHLIA** *turns toward the audience.*)

DAHLIA. (*Enraged.*) Who the hell is that? *Off*, people!

MARCUS. (*Steps aside to answer his phone.*) Hey! Yep, everything's still fine, Chief. He'll be here in...twenty minutes? Okay...okay...bye.

STEPH. Who keeps calling?

> *(Aside.)*

I'm back.

MARCUS. That's for me to know, Steph, and you to never know. Miss Lewis, the notebook! Now!

BARRETTE. Take it. I haven't even had a chance to see what was inside.

> **(MARCUS** *grabs the book and starts flipping through it.* **DAHLIA** *tries to read over his shoulder;* **MARCUS** *catches her in the act, inciting her to clumsily dance away.)*

DAHLIA. *(To* **BARRETTE.***)* Hussy.

MARCUS. Patience, everyone, please. I see he had a strange shorthand.

> **(STEPH** *turns the book [***MARCUS***'s hand] right-side up and* **MARCUS** *immediately gasps.)*

STEPH. Who's it about, Detective?

MARCUS. *(Reading aloud.)* "It's time to unmask... Dr. Griff!"

DR. GRIFF. Whhhut?

MARCUS. "Tell the whole sordid story of how this seemingly sweet psychiatrist sold his patients' secrets to me in exchange for a glowing depiction in one of my novels."
(To **DR. GRIFF.***)* You told Whitney our secrets? So that's how he gathered the information for his books!

STEPH. Obviously! Keep reading.

MARCUS. I was planning on it, Steph, but now it looks like I'm only doing it because you told me to. Jeez.

> *(Reading.)*

"But Dr. Griff seems to be running out of secrets for me. That leaves only one story left to tell: his."
(Sternly.) Anything to say for yourself, Doctor?

DR. GRIFF. *(Unraveling.)* I thought we got each other, Marcus! But I guess you're just like the rest of 'em. He's bananas. She's bananas. You're bananas.

MARCUS & DR. GRIFF. *All of Them Bananas*!

DR. GRIFF. Every day, nod, squint, smile, ask questions, but did anybody ever ask about me? Did anyone ever wanna sing a friendship song with me? At least Arthur Whitney showed me the time of day. The rest of you were too busy complaining! "I have daddy issues," "I get sad when it rains," "I'm gonna kill Arthur Whitney."

MARCUS. Somebody said "I'm gonna kill Arthur Whitney"? Who was it?

DR. GRIFF. You hurt me, Marcus.

MARCUS. If you don't tell me, I'm going to have to bring you down to the station. There's no denying you've got a heck of a motive.

　　　(**DR. GRIFF** *doesn't budge.*)

You might want to call your lawyer, Doctor.

DR. GRIFF. My lawyer-doctor?

MARCUS. Or you could just tell me who said, "I'm gonna kill Arthur Whitney!"

DR. GRIFF. I only reveal secrets during friendship songs!

MARCUS. Oh do you?

[MUSIC NO. 14 "A FRIEND LIKE YOU"]

　　　(**DR. GRIFF** *and* **MARCUS** *stare one another down. Maintaining eye contact,* **MARCUS** *slides over to the piano.*)

　　　(*Slowly at first.*)

WHEN I'M MEETIN' SOME RESISTANCE
THERE'S NO DOUBT I'LL FIND ASSISTANCE
FROM A FRIEND LIKE YOU

　　　(**DR. GRIFF** *turns away but is clearly listening.*)

WHEN A CASE IS GETTIN' MESSY
AND I'M FEELIN' S-O-SY
YOUR SUPPORT WILL PULL ME THROUGH

　　　(**DR. GRIFF** *begins tapping his foot.*)

MURDER NEVER SEEMS ALARMING

WHEN MY ARM IS ARM-IN-ARMING
WITH A PAL WHO'S ALWAYS TRUE
SURE, THE PLOT IS BOUND TO THICKEN
BUT MY PULSE'LL NEVER QUICKEN
'CAUSE I'M STICKIN' WITH A FRIEND LIKE YOU

DR. GRIFF. You're only saying that to get me to talk.

MARCUS. No!

EV'RY BONE OF MINE COULD SHATTER
BUT IT REALLY WOULDN'T MATTER
WITH A FRIEND LIKE YOU

DR. GRIFF. I don't know.

MARCUS.

VI'LENT DEATH CAN BE A DOOZY
BUT MY SONGS ARE NEVER BLUESY
'CAUSE WITH YOU, I CAN'T STAY BLUE

DR. GRIFF. I *wanna* believe.

MARCUS.

SURE, THE KILLER COULD DEFEAT ME
KNOCK ME DOWN AND START TO BEAT ME
BUT I'LL LAUGH UNTIL THEY'RE THROUGH
HA HA HA HA HA!
'CAUSE I WON'T BE GETTIN' TESTY
WHILE I'M JESTIN' WITH MY BESTIE
YEAH, I'M BLESSED TO HAVE A FRIEND LIKE YOU

DR. GRIFF.

FOR TRUE?

MARCUS.

YEP!

A FRIEND WON'T
EVER LEAVE YA HANGING
WHEN THE DAY BRINGS STRESS
A FRIEND SAYS YES
'CAUSE A SECRET IS SWELL
WHEN YOU NEVER DON'T TELL

SO IF TROUBLE SHOULD DESTROY ME
IT WON'T BOTHER OR ANNOY ME

DR. GRIFF.
> WITH A FRIEND LIKE ME?

MARCUS.
> YOU!

MARCUS & DR. GRIFF.
> US!
> THERE'S NO NEED TO DROWN IN SORROW
> IF YOUR LEGS SHOULD BREAK TOMORROW
> 'CAUSE FOR YOU, I'D BREAK MINE TOO

DR. GRIFF. I love you!

> NO DILEMMA WILL DISSUADE YOU
> WITH YOUR CHUM AROUND TO AID YOU

MARCUS.
> AND TO HELP ME CRACK EACH CLUE

DR. GRIFF.
> WE'LL BE B-F-FS FOREVER

MARCUS.
> THAT'S REDUNDANT, BUT WHATEVER

MARCUS & DR. GRIFF.
> I'M SO GLAD TO HAVE A FRIEND LIKE YOU

DR. GRIFF.
> OKAY, I'LL TELL YA

MARCUS & DR. GRIFF.
> GLAD TO HAVE A FRIEND LIKE YOU

MARCUS.
> I'M GLAD TO HEAR IT

MARCUS & DR. GRIFF.
> GLAD TO HAVE A FRIEND... LIKE...

MARCUS. Your big secret, Dr. Griff?

DR. GRIFF. After the big finish, buddy.

MARCUS & DR. GRIFF.
> YOU!
> ONE, TWO, THREE! YEAH!

MARCUS. Go ahead, Doctor. Who said, "I'm going to kill Arthur Whitney"?

DR. GRIFF. Ladies and gentlemen, it's not who *was* exposed, it's...

(Out of breath.)

Sorry, give me a second.

MARCUS. Do you want a sip of your coffee, Dr. Griff?

DAHLIA. I believe he was drinking tea, Detective. Here 'tis.

> **(DAHLIA** *hands the tea to* **MARCUS,** *who hands it to* **DR. GRIFF.***)*

DR. GRIFF. *(Takes a sip.)* Very good. As I was saying, it's not who *was* expo –

> *(He starts immediately into death throes.)*

MARCUS. Dr. Griff! Are you okay?

DR. GRIFF. The tea!

MARCUS. The tea! It must have been...oh no!

> **(DR. GRIFF** *collapses.* **MARCUS** *kneels beside him.)*

It's okay, Dr. Griff. Can you speak?

> **(DR. GRIFF** *shakes his head.)*

Not at all?

> **(DR. GRIFF** *shakes his head.)*

Not even a little syllable or two? To tell me who the killer is?

DR. GRIFF. No, but could I have some music while I die?

> **(MARCUS** *starts to walk toward the piano.)*

DR. GRIFF. Don't leave me!

MARCUS. Well, who's gonna...

> **(THE SUSPECTS** *and* **MARCUS** *both turn to the audience with devilish grins.* **THE SUSPECTS** *grabs somebody from the audience and puts them in the dying* **DR. GRIFF** *position, then goes to the piano.)*

[MUSIC NO. 15 "A FRIEND LIKE YOU (REPRISE)"]

There, there, Dr. Griff. Take it easy. You're being a brave soldier trying to sit up straight. Go ahead, relax.

Let your body go limp. That's right, Doctor. I know sometimes when you're almost dead it helps to stick your tongue out a little. Why don't you go ahead and do that. There we go. If you feel like going into a few violent death spasms you just go for it.

> (*Then, depending on their reaction, he says either, "Good work, Doctor!" or "No? Okay."*)

THOUGH YOUR MOUTH IS GETTIN' BLOODY
GRIFF, YOU'LL ALWAYS BE MY BUDDY
I'M SO GLAD I HAD A FRIEND LIKE YOU

> (**MARCUS** *leads the audience member back to their seat.*)

Ladies and gentlemen, we have a second victim.

DAHLIA. Third! We've already seen the slow, painful death of the American theater. Back me up, people!

MARCUS. Quit changing the subject.

MURRAY. I for one think it's high time we all got the hell out of this slaughterhouse.

MARCUS. Stop panicking. Nobody else will die if you all follow my lead.

BARRETTE. No, Murray's right! I feel very unsafe, especially with me in the room.

BARB. What if I'm next, Detective?

MURRAY. Yes, what if Barb kills one of *us* next?

MARCUS. If you'd all just settle down, I can get back on track. Now, Mrs. Whitney *did* give Griff the tea.

STEPH. Well, no. She handed it to you; *you* handed it to Dr. Griff!

MARCUS. Don't be crazy, Steph.

TIMMY. Let's be honest: any one of us chumps coulda poisoned that tea whiles we's was in the kitchen.

MARCUS. Okay, I can't necessarily prove who poisoned the tea. But we can avoid another death, as long as nobody else drinks any.

STEPH. What if the killer just goes crazy and starts strangling people because they're, I don't know, too cute?

YONKERS. Yikes!

> (**YONKERS** *makes a super-cute face.*)

MARCUS. Which is exactly why we need to get you three boys out of here.

TIMMY. What?

MARCUS. I said one more death and you're out.

> (*To* **LOU.**) Take 'em outside, will ya, Lou?
>
> (*To the* **BOYS.**) Don't worry, Lou will keep you entertained. He's always doing wacky things.

TIMMY. All right, but don't forget, you ever need anything, you just whistle. You know how to whistle, don't you? Show 'im, Yonkers.

YONKERS. You just put your lips togedda and –

MARCUS. I know how to whistle! Now, outside with Officer Lou!

> (*The* **BOYS** *exit.* **MARCUS**'s *cell phone rings once again.* **DAHLIA** *approaches the audience, beside herself with rage.*)

DAHLIA. (*Screaming.*) Who the hell is that? Who do you think you are? This is the theatre. How dare you! We have forgotten our manners!

MARCUS. Mrs. Whitney!

> (**MARCUS** *holds up his cell phone.* **DAHLIA** *sees it for the first time.*)

DAHLIA. (*To the audience.*) It was him.

MARCUS. (*Steps aside to answer his phone.*) Hey! Yep, everything's still fine, Chief. He'll be here in...ten minutes? Okay...okay...bye.

STEPH. Well, what now, Detective? If we don't get this wrapped up soon, we'll have another dead body on our hands. My aunt is getting dangerously close to drinking that tea!

MARCUS. Mrs. Whitney!

DAHLIA. (*Holding the tea cup to her lips.*) What?

MARCUS. That's poisoned!

DAHLIA. *(Putting it down, frustrated.)* Okay. We need to put a sign on it, or we need to throw it out. But leaving it here looking delicious, that's the real crime. That's the real crime.

MARCUS. All hope isn't lost. We at least know that the killer was one of Dr. Griff's patients.

    (Laughing.)

So as long as you weren't all –

(Immediately.) You were all patients, weren't you? Great.

    *(**THE SUSPECTS** becomes a character we haven't met yet, **HENRY VIVALDI**.)*

HENRY VIVALDI. Except for me, Detective!

MARCUS. Wait, who are you?

HENRY VIVALDI. I'm Henry Vivaldi, a proud local firefighter.

MARCUS. Where have you been?

HENRY VIVALDI. The bathroom.

MARCUS. And you weren't a patient of Dr. Griff's?

HENRY VIVALDI. Why would I need to see a psychiatrist? I'm the happiest fireman in the world!

[MUSIC NO. 16 "HENRY VIVALDI"]

    I DESIRE NOTHING HIGHER
    THAN THE FUN OF FIGHTING FIRE
    IN THE GREAT BIG –

MARCUS. Okay, great. You can go.

HENRY VIVALDI. Okay! Tell Mr. Whitney I said happy –

    (Looks at body.)

What's that? Oh no! Tell me that isn't –

    *(**HENRY VIVALDI** kneels beside the body.)*

He's dead? And you're all just standing here? Why did no one fetch me? And why didn't anyone have the decency to cover his face? The flies have got him now! Crawling and crawling.

(To the body.) Oh dear, dear friend. You shall be missed!

AS YOU TRAVEL DOWN THAT WINDING ROAD TO JORDAN
JEREMIAH'S GONNA LEAD YOU ON YOUR WAY
HOLD YOUR –

MARCUS. Okay. We're clearly all dealing with this tragedy in different ways. I need you to excuse yourself.

HENRY VIVALDI. Who are you to order us around? Don't you understand? This man lived. How many of you can say you lived?

YOU ALL SIT HERE ON TOP OF YOUR CASTLE
THINKING THAT YOU RULE THE WORLD
BUT OTHER PEOPLE LIVE, AND OTHER PEOPLE –

MARCUS. Excuse me. Henry? I really need you to go.

HENRY VIVALDI. Oh, I'm going to go. I'm going to pray for your souls. Make no mistake: you've turned this farce into a tragedy. Shame, shame, shame!

> *(He exits dramatically. **DAHLIA** waves goodbye to him.)*

DAHLIA. He is *fun.*

MARCUS. But that still leaves the rest of you. And I'm afraid everyone who saw Dr. Griff is still under suspicion of murder.

STEPH. But Detective, that makes you a suspect too.

MARCUS. Excuse me?

STEPH. Well, earlier, Dr. Griff let it slip that you were a patient of his.

MARCUS. Well, that doesn't prove a thing. It's required for every cop on the force to see a psychiatrist.

STEPH. Detective, you saw Griff. You had a secret revealed in a story. Under your own guidelines, that makes you as much of a suspect as the rest of us.

MARCUS. Except he was shot in the forehead. Was I in the room? 'Cause I'd love to hear how someone from outside this room shot Arthur Whitney in the forehead.

STEPH. It just seems like you're running out of clues, so –

MARCUS. The only thing I'm running out of is patience for your incessant rattling on.

(*Beat, nervously looks at watch.*)

Now, final step according to protocol: reenact the exact moment of the crime. I want you all to go back to your hiding places from earlier.

(**BARRETTE** *leaps into a preposterous position.*)

Really, Barrette? That's how you were hiding?

BARRETTE. It was so dark I thought I'd get some stretching done. You might say I was killing two birds with – no, don't say that.

MARCUS. Gotcha. Mrs. Whitney?

(**DAHLIA** *goes into her hiding pose.*)

Now. Pretend I'm Arthur Whitney returning home and do exactly what you did earlier this evening.

(**MARCUS** *steps outside, then slowly walks back in.*)

Hello, I'm –

DAHLIA. (*Pointing finger gun.*) Bang!

(*Long beat as* **MARCUS** *stares at* **DAHLIA**.)

MARCUS. That's what you did earlier this evening?

DAHLIA. No. I forgot, so I made something up.

MARCUS. Oh for Pete's sake!

(*Light bulb.*)

Can you at least tell me where you saw the flash from the gunshot?

(*Beat.*)

Someone must have seen a flash.

(*Beat, bellowing.*)

Nobody?

(*Beat.*)

Okay. Well, protocol says –

STEPH. Protocol *said* that was the final step, right? So you must have all the information you need.

MARCUS. You're right, Steph, I must. Protocol wouldn't lead me astray. So if I could please have a little silence while I examine the facts, I should have no difficulty exposing the killer.

DAHLIA. Detective, I just remembered something incredibly relevant to the case.

MARCUS. *(Hesitantly.)* You did?

DAHLIA. Yeah. It definitely wasn't Murray.

MARCUS. What?

DAHLIA. Well he told me earlier this evening that he doesn't even like ice cream. So why –

MARCUS. Dahlia.

> *(Beat.)*

Sit.

> *(DAHLIA sits at the piano.)*

MARCUS. Thank you for that perfect example of what I *don't* want to happen. Okay? I'm serious. Be quiet.

> *(DAHLIA mimes locking her closed mouth with a key, which she then offers to MARCUS. She teases him with it but eventually lets him have it. Then, when he's not looking, she swiftly pulls a spare key from her pocket and unlocks her mouth.)*

[MUSIC NO. 17 "PROCESS OF ELIMINATION"]

IF YOU CAN JUST STAY QUIET
THIS WILL ALL MAKE SENSE IN THREE MINUTES

> *(Looks at watch.)*

It has to. Now, time for a little process of elimination.
YOU ALL PLAYED A PART
SO WE CAN START BY ELIMINATING... NONE OF YOU
Very good.

YOU'RE EACH IN A BOOK
WHICH TENDS TO LOOK LIKE AN INDECISIVE CLUE
But wait!
SINCE THE GUN WAS FOUND HERE
IT'S VERY CLEAR IT WAS PLANTED THERE BY... ONE OF
    YOU
WE HAVE THE "WHY" AND THE "HOW"
SO AS OF NOW, LET'S STAY FOCUSED ON THE "WHO"

DAHLIA.

WHO AM I TO ARGUE BUT I'M PRETTY SURE THE KNIFE
    WAS NEVER FOUND

MARCUS. There's no knife! He was shot! And I thought
I told you –

DAHLIA. Sorry! I'm being quiet. We all are. Because we
respect you.

MARCUS. Let me see. What do we know about the guilty
party?

THE KILLER IS SHREWD
SO LET'S CONCLUDE THEY'RE UNLIKELY TO CONFESS TO
    ME

MURRAY.

I'LL CONFESS TO BEING BORED

MARCUS. Shh!

THEY POISONED THE TEA
SO LET'S AGREE THAT THE KILLER HAS... AN ARM

BARRETTE. So what if I do?

MARCUS & STEPH. Shh!

STEPH. He's talking. God.

MARCUS.

THEY WENT THROUGH WITH THE DEED
WHICH AS A LEAD, REALLY COULDN'T MATTER LESS TO
    ME

BARB.

SORRY,
I have to go to the bathroom.

MARCUS.

BUT WHITNEY'S BRAINS
WERE BLOWN OUT

MARCUS.

SO THERE'S NO DOUBT
THAT THE KILLER MEANT
HIM –

Stop!

MURRAY.

Has it been five minutes?

BARB.

Can it, you fat prick!

MURRAY.

CHARMING EXPLANATION
BUT I'M TELLING YOU
THE GUILTY ONE IS
HER!

MARCUS. Murray, you're not helping!

(*Looks at watch.*)

Oh my God, one minute.

DAHLIA. I can help!

MARCUS. Oh no.

DAHLIA. Oh yeah! I'll sing my
"everyone be quiet" song.

QUIET, QUIET, QUIET
EV'RYONE BE QUIET
EV'RYONE BE QUIET
TONIGHT
THAT'S RIGHT
AND IF YOU CAN'T BE
QUIET
I'LL TELL YOU TO BE
QUIET
TILL EVERYONE IS QUIET
ALL RI-I-I-IGHT

MARCUS. No. No. Stop. Is this
really happening? This is
actually happening.

I refuse to compete with
you. Why are you doing
this? Fine, I'll just keep
going.

(**MARCUS** *closes his eyes and plugs his ears.
He continues singing while* **THE SUSPECTS**
alternately sings and screams.)

MARCUS.

AH!
YOU HATED HIM SO

DAHLIA.

OH
QUIET, QUIET, QUIET

MARCUS.
WHICH GOES TO SHOW,
HE WAS KILLED 'CAUSE

SOMEONE HATED HIM

NOW WE'RE GETTIN'
  SOMEWHERE
IT'S SAFE TO ASSUME

THIS VERY ROOM IS THE
  PLACE IT ALL TOOK
  PLACE

LA LA LA LA LA LA

HE'D HAVE DIED ON HIS
  OWN
IF HE HAD KNOWN WHO
  WAS HERE AND WHAT
  AWAITED HIM

HENRY VIVALDI.
I FORGOT MY HAT.

MARCUS.
AAARGH!
WITH PEOPLE YELLING
  NONSTOP
HOW CAN A COP HOPE TO
  EVER SOLVE A CASE
IF NO ONE LISTENS THEN
  IT'S HARD TO BE

BARRETTE.
DAHLIA, STOP JABBERING

STEPH.
EVERYONE, SHH!

BARRETTE.
WHO?

STEPH.
YOU! QUIET! GOD

DAHLIA.
SO! EV'RYONE BE QUIET
  TONIGHT

MURRAY.
YOU'RE THE ONE WHO'S
  ALWAYS TALKING, BARB

BARB.
SHUT UP, MURRAY!
Shut the fuck up!

STEPH.
YOU GUYS HAFTA LET HIM
  TALK
WE HAFTA WORK
  TOGETHER. GOD!

DAHLIA.
ALL RIGHT
YA BETTER NOT MAKE A
  PEEP
WE GOTTA KEEP BEING
  ABSOLUTELY QUIET
SO HE KNOWS THAT WE
RESPECT HIM AND WE

MARCUS.	DAHLIA.
EFFECTIVE	WISH HIM ALL THE BEST
AND I KIND OF GOTTA	AS HE CONTINUES
HURRY IF I WANNA MAKE	
DETECTIVE	

(Beat.)

MARCUS.
AND BY "WANNA MAKE DETECTIVE"
I DON'T MEAN I'M NOT DETECTIVE
ALL I MEAN IS I'M A...
I'M A...
I'M...

I'm sorry. Sorry everyone. I've wasted everybody's time.

STEPH. What are you talking about?

MARCUS. I'm not the detective.

DAHLIA.
WE WERE QUIET
AND LOOK WHAT HAPPENED
I'LL NEVER BE QUIET AGAIN

STEPH. I don't get it.

MARCUS. I'm sure you have a million questions as always, Steph, and I'm sure the real detective will be happy to answer them when he gets here.

STEPH. Real detective?

MARCUS. Detective Grayson should be here in...

(Looks at watch.)

A minute ago. Where is he?

MURRAY. So just to be clear, we've spent the last hour being questioned by...what? Some nobody?

MARCUS. Pretty much.

DAHLIA. And just so *I'm* clear, I've spent the last hour waiting for ice cream that may or may not be found? I haven't been this angry since last week when I found the ballerina's tutu in my underwear drawer...steada in my tutu drawer, where it belongs!

STEPH. Wait a second! Detective! Uh... Officer...may I?

MARCUS. Go for it. What does it matter now?

[MUSIC NO. 18 "STEPH'S SOLUTION (UNDERSCORE)"]

STEPH. Hi, everybody. Okay. If it was *last week* that my aunt Dahlia found that tutu in her underwear drawer, then she must've known about her husband's affair with that bombastic ballerina long before tonight. Plus, my aunt Dahlia planned this whole party herself. And what better way for a jealous wife to cast suspicion elsewhere than to invite a roomful of people who also wanted her husband dead? And don't forget, the tea leaves come from her garden, which is probably some sort of clue too, right? Dahlia Whitney did it all.

> *(Beat, to* **MARCUS**.*)*

Whaddya think?

> *(***MARCUS*** *stands, looking at* **STEPH** *in a brand new light.)*

MARCUS. Wow. Steph. I think you just finished your thesis.

> *(Turns.)*

Mrs. Whitney, your niece here makes a pretty solid case.

DAHLIA. *(Menacingly.)* She also makes a killer omelet.

MARCUS. *(Back to* **STEPH**.*)* Still, until you get a confession, you can't be –

DAHLIA. Oh no, she's right. I did it. Good girl. I did it all. You're listenin' now, aren'tcha? I'm a murderess. Hotcha. Whoopee.

> *(***DAHLIA*** *limps sensuously over to the piano. Instead of playing, however, she pulls a remote control out of the piano bench.)*

Jazz.

> *(She presses a button on the remote, cueing music and some very dramatic lighting.)*

[MUSIC NO. 19 "STEPPIN' OUT OF THE SHADOWS"]

I think m'big song is gonna explain everything.

(She indicates for **MARCUS** *to have a seat.)*

I LIVED M'LIFE IN THE SHADOWS
I NEVER FELT THE SUN
I KNEW THE MOMENT WE MARRIED
THAT M'LIMELIGHT LIFE WAS DONE
SO ALL THESE YEARS I'VE SCRUBBED AND SERVED
PREPARED HIS MEALS AND BRUSHED HIS TEETH
WELL WHO'D HAVE THUNK THAT UNOBSERVED
THERE WAS A MONSTER LURKING BENEATH
THAT'S RIGHT, A MONSTER LURKING BENEATH

BUT NOW AT LONG LAST I'M STEPPIN' OUT OF THE
   SHADOWS
SO SUN, GET READY TO SHINE
MAKE NO MISTAKE, I'M TAKIN' THE STAGE
AND EV'RY FRONT PAGE IS GONNA BE MINE ALL MINE
FINALLY I WON'T FEEL SO INVISIBLE
FINALLY I WON'T LOOK SO INVISIBLE
FINALLY I'LL STEP UP SO THE PLANET CAN SEE
NOTHING'S GONNA STEP ON [ME] –

*(***MARCUS*** takes the remote and presses it, turning off the music.)*

MARCUS. I don't know, Steph. While your reasoning is sound, we can't dismiss the fact that this whole thing feels a little like –

DAHLIA. Ha!

*(***DAHLIA*** has pulled another remote out of the piano bench. She presses it; music and lights start anew.* ***MARCUS*** tries using his remote, but nothing happens.)*

Joke's on you; that one don't work!

MARCUS. But I just –

DAHLIA. As I was saying...

*(During her next verse, **MARCUS** chases **DAHLIA** around the room, trying to get the working remote back.)*

I WAS THE QUEEN OF HIS CASTLE
I PLAYED THE PERFECT WIFE
THEN I GOT MAD FOR SOME REASON
SO I STABBED HIM WITH THAT KNIFE

MARCUS. He was *shot!* Gimme that remote!

DAHLIA.

SO LOCK ME UP AND LOSE THE KEY
GO RIGHT AHEAD, INFORM THE PRESS
AND TELL THEM FOLKS WHO MAKE TV
THAT I'M A REAL BIG BAD MURDERESS
YEAH, I'M A BIG BAD MURDERING MESS... YES!
AND CLEAR THE DECKS 'CAUSE I'M STEPPIN' OUT OF THE –
[SHADOWS SO WORLD, YOU BETTER PREPARE]

*(**MARCUS** successfully gets the other remote and turns the music off.)*

MARCUS. Very good, Mrs. Whitney! Thank you for that!

DAHLIA. I ain't done!

MARCUS. Oh yes you are!

*(Irate, **DAHLIA** hobbles far upstage, searching for something.)*

It's pretty clear that this confession is nothing more than a sad, pathetic attempt for recognition, which –

*(**DAHLIA** finds what she's looking for, an emergency lever that's been situated on the theater's back wall the whole time, and pulls it. The music and lights come back louder and crazier than before. While she proceeds, **MARCUS** tries to do everything he can to stop the music: pulling the lever, unplugging random "offstage" cords and cables, etc., all of which does nothing.)*

DAHLIA.

 I SAID NOTHING'S GONNA STEP
 I SAID NOTHING'S GONNA STEP
 I SAID NOTHING'S GONNA STEP ON ME, BABY
 'CAUSE I MURDERED M'HUSBAND

DAHLIA.	**MARCUS.**
I SAID NOTHING'S GONNA STEP	Yeah, this is a classic case of this kind of thing. As you can see. If I know anything about these patterns, she'll continue to...yeah.
NNNNOTHING'S GONNA STEP	
NUH-NUH-NUH-NOTHING'S GONNA STEP ON ME, BABY	
YA BETTER NOT...	
STEP	
STEP ON	
STEP ON ME	

MARCUS. Okay, what do we do?

DAHLIA.

 NOTHING'S GONNA STEP ON ME!
 OH, FINALLY I WON'T FEEL SO INVISIBLE

MARCUS.	**DAHLIA.**
Invisible... Invisible... It's not who *was* exposed...!	FINALLY I WON'T LOOK SO INVISIBLE

DAHLIA.

 FINALLY I WON'T BE SO INVISIBLE
 FINALLY, WHO? WHAT? ME? NO, INVISIBLE!

MARCUS. Hold everything!

DAHLIA.

 DON'TCHA CALL ME INVISIBLE
 'CAUSE I AIN'T INVISIBLE

  (While **DAHLIA** *continues riffing,* **MARCUS** *smashes everything around him, finally destroying the source of the music. The music and dramatic lighting fizzle out.)*

DAHLIA. How dare you! I had two more choruses...

MARCUS.   DAHLIA.

Hold on...just relax...   And a C-section to get
                                 through!

It's not –

> (**DAHLIA** *throws one of the remotes offstage.*
> *A cat yowls.*)

MARCUS. It's not Mrs. Whitney, everyone!

MURRAY. Why should we listen to a glorified security
guard? Let's just wait for the real detective.

MARCUS. Shut it, Murray! It takes more than a badge to be
a detective.

> (**MARCUS** *removes his badge and throws it*
> *offstage. A louder, angrier cat yowls.*)

It also takes more than a blind allegiance to protocol. It
takes guts, intuition, and sometimes it takes a partner
like Steph here to help you think things through.

(To STEPH.*)* Whaddya say? Will you help me?

STEPH. You want my...help?

MARCUS. *(Whispering.)* Follow my lead.

> *(Back to normal.)*

Nobody saw a flash from the gunshot. Impossible,
right? Not if Arthur Whitney was shot from outside.

STEPH. But he was shot in the forehead. It had to come
from inside the room, remember?

MARCUS. Unless...we missed something earlier. Arthur
Whitney was carrying twenty large books.

> (**STEPH***'s eyes widen. As she puts the pieces*
> *together,* **MARCUS** *slinks toward the back*
> *of the room and slowly pulls out his gun,*
> *making it clear that* **STEPH** *is being used to*
> *distract the room while* **MARCUS** *prepares to*
> *pounce on the killer.*)

STEPH. Of course! If I were carrying twenty large books, I'd
turn the knob, and push the door open with my back...
like this.

*(STEPH reenacts backing in through the door
with the books.)*

Exposing my forehead to anybody who happened to
follow me home.

(Gasps.)

It wasn't one of us! It was someone from outside! And
wait! Dr. Griff's dying words. It's not who *was* exposed;
it's who wasn't. And that can only be –

*(MARCUS pounces on the invisible LOU. He
gets pushed off, however, and LOU grabs
STEPH, putting a gun to her head. MARCUS
slowly stands up and raises his own gun.)*

MARCUS. Put down the gun... Lou.

(LOU cocks the gun and STEPH tightens.)

Easy, Lou!

(STEPH gets dragged to the piano.)

[MUSIC NO. 20 "MARCUS'S SOLUTION (UNDERSCORE)"]

Well, I'm glad you asked. Mrs. Whitney said something
about feeling invisible, and that's when I remembered
that you were the only person here tonight who was
never a character in one of Arthur Whitney's books.

STEPH. "It's not who *was* exposed; it's who *wasn't!*"

*(STEPH gets yanked back. LOU fires his gun
and a vase explodes.)*

MARCUS. It bothered you, Lou, didn't it? You desperately
wanted attention. That's why you were always acting so
wacky. You were trying to give him something to write
about.

STEPH. But despite your nonstop wackiness, he just kept
ignoring you until finally you couldn't take it any
longer!

*(Again, STEPH gets yanked and LOU fires his
gun.)*

MARCUS. Dude!

DAHLIA. Step back, Moscowicz, I got this. I once took a course in hostage situations. Lou. *Ou est la gare?* Oh, wait, that was a French class.

> (**LOU** *fires his gun and* **DAHLIA** *staggers back.*)

DAHLIA. It's okay, he got me in m'throat!

> (*Knocks on her throat.*)

Pure silver.

MARCUS. You told your psychiatrist how upset you were, and when Dr. Griff put two and two together, you snuck over and poisoned the tea. We all knew Griff was the only one drinking any.

> (**LOU** *fires again. Another explosion.*)

You've done a lot of wacky things, Lou, but this one takes the – *cocktail umbrella!*

> (**STEPH** *elbows* **LOU** *and ducks out of the way.* **MARCUS** *runs after him but gets knocked down.* **STEPH** *points toward the door.*)

STEPH. He's getting away!

> (*They run to the window.*)

MARCUS. Look, he's out on the lawn! Quick, help me get this window open.

> (**MARCUS** *and* **STEPH** *throw open a window.*)

Timmy! Boys!

[MUSIC NO. 21 "DON'T FORGET (UNDERSCORE)"]

> (*Dreamy music as* **MARCUS** *remembers the* **BOYS**' *instructions.*)

TIMMY. *(Voice-over.)* Don't forget: you ever need anything...

YONKERS. *(Voice-over.)* You just put your lips togedda and –

MARCUS. Blow!

> (**MARCUS** *whistles out the window.* **TIMMY** *heroically springs into action.*)

TIMMY. That's our cue, gang! Get him!

STEPH. They're tackling him!

MARCUS. Yeah, I know. I can see.

STEPH. Sorry. Sometimes when I get nervous I say what I'm seeing out loud. Look, they've pinned him to the ground and they're scratching at him like a pack of rabid dogs!

MARCUS. That's enough, boys! Bring him in!

STEPH. Look, they're dragging him back inside. Look, they're back inside.

MARCUS. Nice work, boys.

YONKERS. Aw, bananas!

MARCUS. It takes a lot of courage to tackle a hardened criminal like Lou here.

TIMMY. Well we seen a lot woise.

> *(MARCUS and TIMMY share a laugh.)*

MARCUS. You crazy kids. As for you, Officer, you're going away for a long time.

> *(MARCUS handcuffs LOU.)*

You know, there's still one piece of the puzzle that doesn't make sense. How'd you manage to kill Whitney from outside, then plant the murder weapon in the middle of the room without anybody noticing?

> *(A long beat as LOU explains. MARCUS and STEPH listen intently, then gasp in unison.)*

MARCUS & STEPH. Ohhh!

MARCUS. Well, that explains everything! Brilliant, Lou. Brilliant.

DAHLIA. I know someone else who's brilliant around here. Hey, everybody, three cheers for *Detective* Marcus.

MARCUS. That's very sweet, Mrs. Whitney, but of course I'm still only *Officer* Marcus. For now.

> *(MARCUS's cell phone rings. DAHLIA initially looks furious, then sees him and chuckles. MARCUS answers it.)*

(Into phone.) Chief? Great news. You can tell Grayson to turn around; I've got the killer. That's right, I solved the crime, saved the day...

(Sotto voce.) And I may have met somebody!

(Back to normal.) By the way, where *is* Detective Grayson? He got shot? Oh no. Is he okay? He's *dead*? Oh my God. Why? How could this happen? He was so – what's that? You need someone to investigate his murder and the fact that I just solved this case impressed you so now you're gonna make me the new detective? For real?

(To the room.) He's for real!

(Into phone.) Well that's fantastic! Poor Detective Grayson! See you soon!

> *(Hangs up.)*

I'm the detective!

> **(DAHLIA** *turns to the audience, encouraging them to applaud.)*

DAHLIA. Yes, clap for him! Clap your hands off! And now, clap for me! Who sang that song.

> **(DAHLIA** *basks in the applause for a moment, then angrily cuts the audience off.)*

Stop it, stop it! We should *not* have to ask.

MARCUS. You know, Mrs. Whitney, as Detective I'm now responsible for choosing an act to perform at the annual policemen's ball.

MARCUS.	**DAHLIA.**
(Building to a bellow.) It's a little fundraiser we do, so if you're interested, we'd love to have your vocal talents for an opening number or something, if you're –! You do that.	*(Bellowing too.)* Am I? Oh my! *Oh my!* This is...! What an honor! Huge honor! I – I gotta start rehearsin'!

BARRETTE. Poor, dear Detective Grayson. He always did have a mild allergy...to bullets.

MARCUS. Barrette?

BARRETTE.

(Drops the act.) I'm kidding! I'm kidding, that's my thing, it's just a... I'm only joking.
(Stops suddenly, with alarming passion.) I love you.

MARCUS.

Okay. Okay, you! I wasn't sure.

MARCUS. Go away.

(Turns.)

Steph?

STEPH. I guess you should probably ship off to the ol' scene of the crime, huh?

[MUSIC NO. 22 "FINALE (I NEED A PARTNER / PROTOCOL SAYS)"]

MARCUS. I have a minute. The chief's got someone keeping an eye on the suspects. So! I guess you won't be driving up from the city as often, with your psychiatrist gone.

STEPH. Yeah, he's dead.

MARCUS. Hey, Steph?

STEPH. Yeah?

MARCUS.

I THINK I NEED A PARTNER

STEPH.

TOGETHER EV'RY DAY

MARCUS.

OR... AN ASSISTANT

STEPH.

EQUAL IN EV'RY WAY

MARCUS.

PERHAPS AT FIRST, AN INTERN

STEPH.

> A DUO
> AND OFF
> THE CLOCK
> WHO KNOWS?

MARCUS.

> YOU'LL PROB'LY START
>   BYHAULING TRASH
>   AND MAKING COFFEE,
>   BUT WHO KNOWS?

MARCUS.

> STEPH, IT'S TRUE
> I NEED A PARTNER LIKE...

> YOU NEED A PARTNER
>   LIKE...

MARCUS & STEPH

> I/YOU NEED A PARTNER...

> *(They lean in to almost kiss.)*

MARCUS.

> ...LIKE YOU

STEPH. Yeah, I got it.

MARCUS. Okay, just making sure. Let's go solve that murder. And maybe afterwards, you and I could grab some donuts?

STEPH. I don't know, Detective. At the end of *Unsolved Hearts*, Jarcus Joscowicz vows to never again let anybody close to *his* heart.

MARCUS. I told you, Steph: that book isn't about me.

> *(They share a laugh.)*

> Goodnight, Murray!

MURRAY. Goodnight.

MARCUS. Barb.

BARB. Okay!

MARCUS. Boys.

TIMMY. So long!

MARCUS. Miss Lewis.

BARRETTE. *Adieu.*

MARCUS. Mrs. Whitney.

DAHLIA. Peace out, sunshine!

MARCUS. Will do. I'll send someone for the bodies.

STEPH. Can I drive, Detective?

MARCUS. Now, Steph, protocol says... Oh, hell with it.

(He throws her the keys.)

I NEED A PARTNER LIKE...

STEPH.

YOU NEED A PARTNER LIKE...

MARCUS.

I NEED A PARTNER WHO UNDERSTANDS THAT
EV'RY PUZZLEPIECE HOLDS A CLUE
WHEN YOU'RE ADDING 'EM UP, JUST DO AS PROTOCOL
   SAYS
YOU'LL SOON SUCCEED
TAKE IT, STEPH

STEPH. Oh!

EV'RY FINGERPRINT FITS A HAND

MARCUS.

THAT'S RIGHT!

STEPH.

I KNOW

IF YOU'RE WILLING TO UNDERSTAND THAT
PROTOCOL WORKS

MARCUS.

YET, BE AWARE

MARCUS & STEPH.

NOTHING COMPARES WITH BEIN' A PAIR
THAT'S THE ONLY PARTNERSHIP YOU NEED!

> *(**THE SUSPECTS** runs away from the piano and becomes **TIMMY**.)*

TIMMY. Well, Yonkers, it looks like we got away with it.

YONKERS. Yeah, Timmy. That certainly was a close call.

TIMMY. Boy, I'll say. We'll have to be much more careful... *the next time we steal the ice cream*! G'night, folks!

> *(**THE SUSPECTS** runs back to the piano. He and **MARCUS** finish the playoff as partners.)*

(Lights.)

[MUSIC NO. 23 "FINALE ULTIMO (A FRIEND LIKE YOU)"]

(After a round of bows, **THE SUSPECTS** *and* **MARCUS** *cross back to the piano and play a four-handed grand finale.)*

[MUSIC NO. 24 "EXIT MUSIC (IT WAS HER / PROTOCOL SAYS)"]

End of Show